Love & War: The Battle of Virginia Beach

Michael Gordon

Published by MG Books, 2024.

This is a work of fiction. Similarities to real people, places, or events are entirely coincidental.

LOVE & WAR: THE BATTLE OF VIRGINIA BEACH

First edition. November 13, 2024.

ISBN: 979-8227496881

Written by Michael Gordon.

Chapter 1

The vibrant energy of Virginia Beach's nightlife pulsed through the air as Brandon Hill, a tall, muscular, young black man with a subtle yet stylish fade, navigated his way through the crowded nightclub. Wearing a gold chain around his neck, a green shirt, jeans, and boots, Brandon felt confident he could meet a woman tonight. His eyes, deep brown and inquisitive, scanned the room, taking in the flashing lights and pulsating beats. But his attention was immediately captured by a vision of pure femininity—Hilary Tork.

Hilary, a curvy beauty with a radiant smile, was a sight to behold in her form-fitting, low-cut dress that accentuated her generous curves. Her brown hair cascaded over her shoulders, framing her face, and her eyes sparkled with a mischievous glint that hinted at her outgoing nature. She moved with effortless grace, her body swaying to the music, drawing Brandon's gaze like a magnet.

Feeling a sudden surge of confidence, Brandon made his way to the bar, his heart pounding with anticipation. He ordered a drink, his hands slightly trembling as he thought about approaching this stunning woman. With the drink in hand, he steeled himself and ventured into the crowd, searching for the captivating Hilary.

He found her in a secluded corner, where the music's intensity softened, allowing for conversation. As he approached, she looked up, her eyes meeting his, and a smile played on her lips. Brandon's voice was soft, his words almost drowned out by the music, but he managed to ask, "Hi, I'm Brandon. Can I buy you a drink?"

Hilary's eyes lit up, and she nodded enthusiastically. "I'd love one, Brandon. I'm Hilary, by the way." Her voice was like velvet, smooth and enticing, sending a shiver down Brandon's spine. They chatted briefly, their drinks clinking together in a silent toast. Hilary's laughter, like a melody, filled the space between them as they discovered a shared love for dancing, travel, and the simple pleasures of pizza and sports.

As the conversation flowed, Brandon felt a growing connection with Hilary. Her wit and charm captivated him, and he found himself drawn to her infectious energy. Before long, they were dancing, their bodies moving in sync, the music becoming a soundtrack to their burgeoning attraction.

Brandon's hands rested gently on Hilary's waist, her skin soft and warm beneath his touch. Her eyes, now sparkling with desire, met his, and she leaned in close, her breath hot against his ear. "You're a great dancer, Brandon," she whispered, her voice laced with seduction. "Let's take this dance somewhere more private."

Brandon's heart raced, his body responding to her suggestion. He nodded, his voice hoarse with desire. "My place is just a few blocks from here. We can go there."

Hilary's eyes widened with anticipation, and without a word, they made their way out of the club, the cool night air doing little to cool their burning desire. Brandon's apartment was a short walk away, and as they arrived, he fumbled with his keys, his hands trembling with excitement.

Once inside, the door closed behind them, sealing them in a private sanctuary of desire. Brandon turned to Hilary, his eyes hungry as he took in her beauty. She stood before him, her dress hugging her curves, and with a slow, deliberate motion, she began to undo the buttons of her dress, revealing a lacy black bra that barely contained her ample cleavage.

Brandon's breath caught in his throat as he reached out, his fingers gently tracing the curves of her waist, then slowly upward, caressing the swell of her breasts. Hilary sighed, her head tilting back, offering her neck to his exploring lips. He kissed her there, his tongue tracing a path that left her shivering with pleasure.

As their passion intensified, Brandon guided Hilary to the bedroom, where they undressed each other with eager hands. Hilary's dress fell to the floor, revealing her hourglass figure, her pale skin glowing in the soft light. Brandon's shirt and pants quickly followed, exposing his bulky, muscular frame.

They fell onto the bed, their bodies entwined, lips locked in a passionate kiss. Brandon's hands roamed over Hilary's body, cupping her full breasts, teasing her nipples until they peaked, hard and erect. She arched into his touch, her hands running through his short hair, urging him on.

Brandon's lips trailed down her body, leaving a trail of kisses along her collarbone and between her breasts. He paused to pay homage to each nipple, sucking and laving them with his tongue, eliciting moans of pleasure from Hilary. She writhed beneath him, her hands guiding his head lower, towards the aching core of her desire.

As Brandon's lips reached the apex of her thighs, Hilary's breath quickened, her body tensing in anticipation. He parted her folds with his thumbs, exposing her glistening pussy, and blew a gentle breath over her sensitive flesh, making her shudder.

"Oh, Brandon," she whispered, her voice thick with need. "Please, don't tease me anymore."

Brandon smiled against her wetness, his breath hot against her skin. He teased her clit with the tip of his tongue, circling it slowly, then flicking it rapidly, driving Hilary wild with desire. She bucked against his mouth, her hands gripping the sheets, as he delved deeper, his tongue sliding inside her, tasting her essence.

Hilary's moans filled the room as Brandon's skilled tongue worked its magic, bringing her closer and closer to the edge. Her hips undulated in rhythm with his licks, her body building towards an explosive climax.

"Brandon, I'm going to cum!" she cried out, her voice breathless.

Brandon redoubled his efforts, his tongue flicking her clit relentlessly, his fingers plunging into her wet heat, stroking her G-spot.

Hilary's orgasm hit her like a wave, crashing over her body, causing her to cry out in ecstasy. Her pussy clenched around his fingers, milking them as her juices flowed, flooding his hand with her essence.

Brandon continued to pleasure her through the waves of her orgasm, his tongue and fingers relentless in their pursuit of her pleasure. As her climax began to subside, he slowly withdrew his fingers, his lips leaving her throbbing clit with a final, tender kiss.

Hilary lay panting, her body sated and blissful, as Brandon moved up her body, his cock hard and straining against her thigh. She reached down, wrapping her hand around his length, stroking him gently.

"Your turn, Brandon," she whispered, her eyes gleaming with desire. "Let me make you feel as good as you just made me feel."

Brandon groaned as Hilary's skilled fingers worked their magic on his cock, stroking and caressing him to full hardness. She leaned down, her lips brushing his ear, her breath hot and tantalizing. "I want to taste you, Brandon. I want to feel you in my mouth."

With that, she took him into her warm, wet mouth, her tongue swirling around the head of his cock, sending shocks of pleasure through his body. Brandon moaned, his hands threading through her hair, urging her on as she took him deep, her throat constricting around his shaft.

Hilary's mouth worked him expertly, her hands cupping his balls, gently massaging them as she sucked and licked him with abandon. Brandon's hips thrust upward, his body seeking release, as she continued to pleasure him, her mouth and hands working in perfect harmony.

"I'm going to cum, Hilary," he gasped, his body tense with the effort of holding back.

Hilary pulled back, her lips glistening with his pre-cum, and smiled up at him. "Not yet. I want you to fill me up first."

With that, she straddled him, guiding his throbbing cock to her entrance. She sank down slowly, her pussy enveloping him, inch by inch, until he was buried deep inside her.

Brandon groaned, his eyes rolling back in his head as he felt her tight, wet heat surrounding him. Hilary began to move, her hips rocking in a slow, sensuous rhythm, her breasts swaying with the motion. Brandon's hands cupped her breasts, his thumbs teasing her nipples, as she rode him, her pussy clenching and releasing his cock in a silken grip.

"Oh, fuck, you feel so good," Brandon groaned, his body arching up to meet her downward thrusts.

Hilary's breath came in short gasps as she quickened her pace, her pussy milking his cock, driving him wild with desire. Brandon's hands gripped her hips, guiding her as she rode him, their bodies moving together in a primal dance.

"I'm close, Brandon," she panted, her voice hoarse with passion. "Cum with me, baby."

Brandon's body tightened, his cock throbbing as he neared his climax. Hilary's pussy clenched around him, her muscles contracting in time with her orgasm, and Brandon couldn't hold back any longer.

"Hilary, I'm cumming!" he cried out, his body convulsing as he filled her with his hot, creamy load.

Hilary's eyes rolled back as she felt his cum spurt inside her, triggering her own climax. She cried out, her body shaking, as wave after wave of pleasure washed over her.

As their orgasms subsided, they collapsed onto the bed, their bodies glistening with sweat, their hearts racing. Brandon held Hilary close, his arms wrapped tightly around her, as they lay in a contented post-coital haze.

The night had been incredible, their connection intense, and as they drifted off to sleep, entwined in each other's arms, neither could have anticipated the events that would unfold in the morning.

The sun had barely risen when a thunderous boom shook the apartment, jolting Brandon and Hilary awake. Hilary, her eyes wide with alarm, clutched Brandon's arm. "What was that?" she asked, her voice trembling.

Brandon, his heart racing, hurried to the window, pulling back the curtains. Outside, the sky was filled with a terrifying sight—jets streaking across the sky, dropping bombs that exploded in fiery bursts.

"We have to get out of here!" Brandon exclaimed, his voice laced with urgency.

Hilary, still half-asleep and disoriented, stumbled out of bed, her eyes darting around the room. "What's happening? Why are they bombing the city?"

Brandon shook his head, his mind racing as he tried to make sense of the chaos unfolding outside. "I don't know, but we need to get to safety. Now!"

Chapter 2

The sun had barely risen, casting a soft, warm glow over the resort city of Virginia Beach, but the peaceful morning light did not reflect the chaos that had erupted. Brandon and Hilary, still reeling from the intensity of their night together, were abruptly thrown into a scene of terror. Dressed hastily, Brandon in his casual jeans and t-shirt, and Hilary, borrowing clothes from Brandon in a baggy pair of jeans and shirt, rushed out of the apartment, their hearts pounding with fear and adrenaline.

As they stepped onto the oceanfront street, the sight before them was surreal and horrifying. The once vibrant beach city streets were now a war zone. The tall apartment and hotel towers were on fire. The smell of the salty ocean air was replaced by smoke, blood and gunpowder. The sound of screams and bullets filled the air. Parachutes dotted the sky, carrying soldiers who descended upon the unsuspecting city. But these were not American troops; their uniforms were unfamiliar, bearing the mark of a foreign power. The soldiers spoke in harsh, guttural tones, their language unmistakably Russian. Brandon's eyes widened in disbelief as he realized the unthinkable was happening—Russia was invading American soil.

"Oh my God, Brandon, what's going on? Who are these people?" Hilary's voice trembled as she clutched his arm, seeking comfort and protection.

"I think... I think Russia is attacking us," Brandon replied, his voice hoarse with shock. "We have to get out of here, now!"

The streets were in pandemonium. Civilians, caught off guard, scrambled for safety, while the Russian soldiers, armed with assault rifles, opened fire without mercy. Bullets whizzed by, shattering windows and piercing through flesh. Brandon's instincts kicked in, and he grabbed Hilary's hand, pulling her close as they darted through the chaos. They had to get to safety, but with every step, the danger seemed to grow.

"This way!" Brandon shouted, leading Hilary down an alleyway, hoping to find cover. As they ran, Brandon's mind raced. He had never imagined himself in a war zone, let alone fighting for his life. He was just a regular guy, an accountant with dreams of becoming a millionaire, not a soldier. But now, he had to protect Hilary, the woman he had only just met but already felt a deep connection with.

Hilary, usually the life of the party, was now a shadow of her former self. The fear in her eyes was evident, but she refused to let it consume her. "We can't just run forever, Brandon. We need a plan. We have to fight back!"

Brandon nodded, appreciating her determination. "You're right. We can't let them take our city, our country, without a fight. But we need weapons. I saw one of the soldiers drop his rifle when he landed. Let's get it, and then we can make our way to the military base. They'll know what to do."

Hilary's eyes narrowed with determination. "Okay, let's do it. I can handle a gun, my dad taught me how to shoot when I was a kid. We'll show them they picked the wrong city to mess with."

Together, they sprinted towards the fallen soldier, their hearts pounding with a mix of fear and anger. As they reached the body, Brandon quickly grabbed the assault rifle, checking the magazine to ensure it was loaded. He handed the weapon to Hilary, who handled it with surprising ease.

"I never thought I'd be holding a gun like this, but I'm ready to use it if I have to," she said, her voice steady.

"Me neither, but we have to do what we can to survive. Let's move towards the base, stay low, and take cover when we can," Brandon instructed, his soft-spoken nature now replaced by a steely determination.

They navigated the streets, ducking behind abandoned cars and crumbling buildings, using whatever cover they could find. The sound of gunfire and explosions echoed through the city, filling the air with smoke and debris. Brandon and Hilary kept their heads down, moving quickly, their eyes scanning for any signs of danger.

As they neared the outskirts of the oceanfront, they spotted a group of American soldiers engaging the Russians in a fierce firefight. Brandon recognized the American flag on their uniforms, and a surge of hope filled him.

"There! That's our military! We need to get to them, they'll help us!" Brandon shouted, urging Hilary forward.

The American soldiers, outgunned and outnumbered, were putting up a valiant fight. Hilary and Brandon joined the battle, taking cover behind a damaged wall and returning fire. Hilary's aim was true, and she took down several Russian soldiers, her determination burning brightly. Brandon, despite his lack of combat experience, held his own, providing covering fire and assisting the pinned down American soldiers.

The battle raged on, and the American soldiers, with the help of Brandon and Hilary, managed to push the Russians back. But the enemy was relentless, and the fighting continued for what felt like an eternity. Brandon's arms ached from firing his weapon, and Hilary's shirt was now torn and covered in dirt and sweat, but they fought on, driven by a sense of duty and the will to survive.

Just as it seemed the Americans were gaining the upper hand, a massive explosion rocked the ground, sending soldiers flying. Brandon and Hilary were thrown to the ground, dazed and disoriented. When they looked up, they saw a Russian tank rolling towards them, its cannon aimed directly at their position.

"We have to move, now!" Brandon yelled, pulling Hilary to her feet. They sprinted towards a nearby abandoned hotel on the boardwalk, their lungs burning with exertion. As they burst through the entrance, they found themselves in a large, empty storeroom.

"We can't stay here, they'll find us!" Hilary panted, her face flushed.

Brandon looked around, his eyes landing on a large, heavy crate. "We can hide in here, it might buy us some time. But we need to be quiet."

They squeezed into the crate, their bodies pressed tightly together. The darkness enveloped them, and they could hear the Russian soldiers searching the area. Brandon's heart was pounding against his ribcage, and he could feel Hilary's rapid breaths on his neck.

"I never thought I'd be in a situation like this," Hilary whispered, her voice trembling. "I just wanted to find a husband, settle down, and have a family. Not fight in a war."

"Me neither," Brandon replied softly. "I always thought I'd have a normal life, a successful career, and a loving family. But now, I'm just grateful we're alive and together."

As they huddled in the darkness, their fears and hopes intertwined, a bond was forming between them, forged in the crucible of war. They were strangers just hours ago, but now, their lives were irrevocably intertwined, their fates linked by this extraordinary night.

The minutes ticked by, each one feeling like an eternity. Finally, the footsteps outside began to fade, and the sound of the Russian soldiers receded. Brandon cautiously peered out of the crate, ensuring the coast was clear.

"I think they're gone," he whispered, helping Hilary out of their hiding place.

They emerged from the warehouse, their eyes scanning the devastated landscape. The battle had moved on, leaving behind a trail of destruction. Brandon and Hilary knew they had to keep moving, to find the American military base and safety.

"We need to stick together," Brandon said, his voice firm. "We're stronger together, and we can make it through this. We'll get to the base, and then..."

"And then we'll see," Hilary finished his sentence, a hint of a smile on her face. "I never thought I'd say this, but I'm glad I met you, Brandon Hill. You're quite the hero."

Brandon blushed, his soft-spoken nature returning. "I'm just doing what anyone would do. We have to look out for each other. But I'm glad I met you too, Hilary. I know last night was just a hookup, but..."

Before Brandon could finish his sentence, a loud explosion interrupted them, sending them running for cover once more. The battle was not over, and Virginia Beach was still under siege.

"Save it for later..." Hilary replied.

Brandon bonded knowing that their day wasn't over. War had broken out and they had to stay together if they wanted to survive. As they fled, hand in hand, they knew their journey was far from over, and their fate remained uncertain.

Chapter 3

As Brandon and Hilary navigated the chaotic streets of Virginia Beach, the morning sun offered little warmth to their fear-stricken hearts. The once lively city had transformed into a war zone, with Russian soldiers swarming every corner. Their journey towards the military base, a haven of safety, was fraught with peril at every turn. The sound of gunfire and explosions echoed through the air, a constant reminder of the danger that lurked around each corner.

The couple's bond, forged in the heat of passion and strengthened by their shared experience, became their anchor amidst the chaos. Brandon, typically a reserved accountant, found himself stepping up in ways he never imagined. His eyes, usually focused on spreadsheets and numbers, now scanned the surroundings with a newfound alertness, seeking a path to safety. Hilary, the vibrant nurse, moved with purpose, her medical expertise becoming their secret weapon.

As they rounded a corner, a chilling sight unfolded before them. A group of civilians, mostly families with young children, cowered in an alley, desperately seeking shelter from the onslaught. Russian soldiers had them cornered, firing indiscriminately, their bullets whizzing dangerously close. It was a scene of sheer terror, and Brandon and Hilary knew they couldn't leave these innocent people to their fate.

Brandon, driven by an innate sense of justice, made a quick decision. "We can't just stand here," he said, his voice steady despite the tremor in his hands. "We have to help them. Hilary, cover me."

Hilary's eyes widened, but she nodded, trusting Brandon's instincts. She took position behind a partially destroyed car, her small frame blending into the shadows. With her heart racing, she readied her pistol, a weapon she had never thought she'd need. Brandon, with surprising agility, darted towards the alley, using the cover of a nearby building to shield himself from the enemy fire.

The Russian soldiers, caught off guard by Brandon's bold move, hesitated for a crucial moment. It was all the time Brandon needed. He reached the terrified civilians, shouting instructions. "Stay low! Follow me, and don't look back!"

The group, urged on by Brandon's commanding presence, scrambled to their feet. Hilary, from her vantage point, provided covering fire, her aim surprisingly accurate as she picked off two soldiers, forcing the others to take cover. Brandon ushered the civilians forward, leading them through a maze of alleys and backstreets, using his knowledge of the city streets to evade the enemy.

As they ran, Hilary noticed a young boy, no older than seven, lagging behind, his small legs struggling to keep up. She darted out from her cover, risking exposure, and swept the boy into her arms. "You're safe now," she whispered, her voice trembling. The boy's tear-streaked face lit up with a fleeting smile, a moment of hope amidst the chaos.

They reached a deserted building, its shattered windows offering a temporary sanctuary. Brandon, with his newfound leadership skills, quickly assessed the situation. "We'll rest here for a while. Hilary, can you tend to the wounded?"

Hilary nodded, her nurse's instincts kicking in. She rummaged through a medical supply bag she found off a dead soldier, producing a small medical kit. "I'll do what I can," she said, her voice steady despite the shaking of her hands.

The group huddled together, their eyes wide with fear and gratitude. Hilary moved among them, her gentle touch and soothing words offering comfort. She cleaned wounds, applied makeshift bandages, and offered painkillers from her limited supply. It was a heartbreaking scene, and Hilary had to make difficult choices. Every time she gave a dose of medication, she knew it was one less for the next person in need.

Brandon, seeing the toll it was taking on Hilary, approached her. "You're doing an incredible job," he said, his voice soft and reassuring. "You're saving lives, Hilary. I'm here for you."

Hilary's eyes met Brandon's, and she felt a wave of gratitude wash over her. In that moment, she realized how much she needed his support. To her it was strange to feel so many feelings for a man she just met yesterday. "Thank you," she whispered, her voice hoarse. "This is... this is hard."

Brandon squeezed her hand, his touch offering silent strength. "We'll get through this together. You're a hero, Hilary. Never forget that."

As the group regained some strength, Brandon formulated a plan. "We can't stay here for long. We need to keep moving. The military base is our best bet for safety."

A sense of determination filled the group, and they prepared to move out once more. Hilary, her medical kit repacked, took a final look at the wounded, hoping her efforts would be enough. As they ventured out, the streets seemed eerily quiet, as if the city was holding its breath.

Their progress was slow, each step a calculated risk. Brandon and Hilary took turns leading the group, their eyes scanning for any sign of danger. As they approached a crossroads, a deafening explosion rocked the ground, sending them tumbling to the ground. Hilary cried out as a shower of debris rained down, the result of a nearby building collapsing.

Brandon scrambled to his feet, reaching out to help Hilary up. "Are you hurt?" he asked, his voice filled with concern.

Hilary shook her head, her hands trembling as she brushed off the dust. "I'm okay," she managed, her voice unsteady. "But we can't stay here. We need to keep moving."

They helped the others up, their fear palpable as they surveyed the destruction around them. Brandon, ever resourceful, led them down a side street, seeking an alternate route. The sun was high in the sky now, its rays offering little comfort as they marched on, driven by a desperate need to reach safety.

As they turned a corner, a group of American soldiers came into view, their weapons drawn, eyes alert. Brandon and Hilary exchanged a look of relief, and they rushed towards the soldiers, their newfound charges in tow.

"We need to get these civilians to safety," Brandon called out, his voice carrying a sense of authority. "We've been under fire, and we have wounded."

The soldiers, their faces hardened by the day's battles, quickly sprang into action. "This way," one of them shouted, leading the group towards a nearby evacuation point.

Hilary, her medical skills still in demand, assisted the soldiers in tending to the wounded. Brandon, meanwhile, kept a watchful eye on the civilians, ensuring their safety. As they reached the evacuation point, a sense of relief washed over them, but it was short-lived.

"We're under attack!" a soldier shouted, his voice cutting through the air.

Brandon and Hilary exchanged a glance, their hearts sinking. The battle had followed them, and they knew they couldn't outrun it forever.

Chapter 4

Brandon and Hilary found themselves in the midst of a tense standoff between the American soldiers and Russians. Their night's passionate encounter seemed like a distant memory as they stood side by side, their hearts pounding in unison with the deafening sound of gunfire. Brandon's palms wear sweaty and his arms were tried from the recoil of the rifle. Never before did he think he could have to kill someone, but now he's claimed over a dozen lives.

Hilary felt the same as she killed another Russian crotched in coverage. Bullets whizzed past her head, but she didn't flinch, she couldn't. She knew one wrong move meant life and death. She had to keep going. She had to live.

The American soldiers, a group of battle-hardened veterans, had welcomed Brandon and Hilary's assistance during the firefight. Despite their lack of military training, the couple had fought bravely, using their wits and determination to hold off the enemy. Brandon, with his quick thinking and strategic mind, had taken charge, directing civilians to safety and providing cover fire. Hilary, her medical skills invaluable, tended to the wounded, ensuring their survival. Their actions had not gone unnoticed either, and in the end, the Americans were able to hold off the ambush by the Russians.

After the firefight was over, a soldier approached Brandon and Hilary.

"You two did great back there," Sergeant Williams, a weathered soldier with a scar across his cheek, acknowledged. "But this isn't a game. It's too risky for civilians to engage directly. We need to get you to the base."

Brandon, his dark eyes flashing with determination, spoke up, "We want to help, Sergeant. We can't just sit back and watch our city burn."

Hilary nodded in agreement, her brown hair falling across her face as she said, "We have to do something. We can't let them take over."

The sergeant's expression softened, understanding the courage it took for these civilians to stand against such odds. "I appreciate your spirit, but we have orders to evacuate you. We'll take you to the base, where you'll be safe. From there, you can assist in other ways."

Before they could argue further, a Humvee roared into view, its tires kicking up dust as it screeched to a halt. The vehicle was packed with heavily armed soldiers, their faces grim. "We've got reinforcements!" one of the soldiers shouted, jumping out of the truck. "Let's move out!"

Sergeant Williams turned to Brandon and Hilary. "This is your ride. We'll take you to the base, and you can help us coordinate from there. We can use your skills, but we need to keep you safe."

As they climbed into the Humvee, the group of civilians they had been protecting followed suit, finding solace in the vehicle's sturdy metal frame. The soldiers briefed them on the situation during the bumpy ride.

"The Russians launched a surprise attack, taking advantage of our reduced defenses. We're still trying to figure out how they managed to slip past our early warning systems," one soldier explained.

"It's almost like someone on the inside helped them," another soldier added, his voice laced with suspicion. "We've got intel that there might be a traitor in our government, someone who's been feeding them information."

Brandon's eyes widened, his mind racing with the implications. "That's impossible! Who would do such a thing?"

Hilary, sitting beside him, placed a comforting hand on his shoulder. "We can't jump to conclusions. It could be a mistake. We need to focus on getting to the base and helping however we can."

The journey to the military base was a tense one, with the Humvee weaving through the city's ruins. They passed abandoned buildings, their windows shattered, and streets littered with debris. The sound of gunfire echoed in the distance, a constant reminder of the ongoing battle.

Suddenly, the peaceful drive turned into a nightmare. An explosion rocked the vehicle, sending it careening towards the sidewalk. The soldiers quickly regained control, but the attack had left them vulnerable. Russian soldiers, having anticipated their route, emerged from the shadows, opening fire on the Humvee.

"Ambush!" Sergeant Williams shouted, returning fire through the open window. "Everyone, get down!"

Brandon and Hilary ducked as bullets pinged off the vehicle's armor. The civilians screamed, cowering in fear. Hilary, her nursing instincts kicking in, tended to a young girl who had been grazed by a bullet.

"We need to get out of here!" Brandon yelled, his voice rising above the chaos. "We're sitting ducks!"

Sergeant Williams nodded, his eyes scanning the surroundings. "We'll make a run for it. Everyone, stay low and follow my lead!"

The soldiers coordinated their exit, providing cover fire as the civilians and Brandon and Hilary scrambled out of the Humvee. They dashed towards an abandoned building, seeking temporary refuge. The Russians pursued, their assault relentless.

Brandon, his heart pounding, grabbed Hilary's hand, pulling her along. "We have to keep moving!"

They sprinted through the building, their footsteps echoing in the vast space. Hilary, despite her fear, maintained her composure, helping a wounded soldier along the way. As they reached the back exit, a Russian soldier appeared, blocking their path.

Without hesitation, Brandon lunged forward, tackling the soldier to the ground. They wrestled, their bodies entwined in a struggle for survival. Brandon, fueled by adrenaline, managed to overpower the enemy, disarming him. Hilary, witnessing the fight, picked up the discarded weapon, aiming it at the Russians who were closing in.

"Get back!" she shouted, her voice trembling. "We won't go down without a fight!"

The Russians, taken aback by the unexpected resistance, hesitated. In that moment of hesitation, American reinforcements arrived, their vehicles roaring into the building. The soldiers, seeing the tide turn, retreated, leaving the battered group to catch their breath.

Sergeant Williams approached Brandon and Hilary, his face a mixture of relief and admiration. "You two are something else. Your bravery bought us time. We'll get you to the base, but we need to move fast. The Russians are adapting their tactics."

As they made their way out of the building, Brandon and Hilary exchanged a glance, their bond strengthened by the shared ordeal. They had faced death together, and their desire to make a difference only grew stronger.

"We'll do whatever it takes to help," Brandon said, his voice steady.

Hilary smiled, her determination unwavering. "We're in this together. Let's show them what we're made of."

As they joined the soldiers, preparing for the next leg of the journey, Brandon and Hilary knew their fight was far from over. The battle for Virginia Beach raged on, and they were determined to play their part, even if it meant defying the odds and challenging the limits of their courage.

The convoy of Humvees sped towards the military base, the soldiers on high alert. The sky above them was filled with the roar of fighter jets, adding an air of urgency to their mission. As they neared the base, the true scale of the invasion became apparent. Tanks and armored vehicles lined the perimeter, a formidable defense against the encroaching enemy.

"We're almost there," Sergeant Williams assured them, his voice carrying above the vehicle's rumble. "Once we're inside, we can assess the situation and plan our next move."

Brandon and Hilary exchanged a glance, their eyes filled with determination and a hint of apprehension. They had come a long way from their passionate night in the city. Since then they used their wits and skills to survive the intense battle with the Russians.

As the Humvees pulled into the base, a sense of organized chaos greeted them. Jets soared above their heads, soldiers scurried about, preparing defenses, while medical teams tended to the wounded. The sight was both reassuring and overwhelming. Brandon and Hilary knew their presence here could make a difference, but the reality of war was starkly different from their previous encounters.

"Follow me," Sergeant Williams instructed, leading them towards a command center. "We'll brief the higher-ups on the situation and see where we can best utilize your skills."

The command center bustled with activity. Maps were spread across tables, and officers discussed strategies, their voices tense. Brandon and Hilary stood by, feeling a mix of awe and insignificance amidst the military elite.

A tall, stern-faced colonel approached them, his eyes assessing. "I'm Colonel Stevens. You must be the civilians who aided our troops. We've heard about your bravery. While you don't have to, the army is putting together a local militia to fight the Russians, would you like to be apart of the militia?"

Brandon and Hilary nodded.

"I feel like it's my duty as an American to say yes." Brandon replied.

"I feel the same. The people of Virginia Beach need us." Hilary added.

"Good, we'll put your skills to good use," Colonel Stevens continued. "Brandon, your knowledge of the city's layout will be invaluable for our intelligence team. Hilary, your medical expertise is desperately needed at the field hospital."

Hilary's eyes lit up at the prospect of helping the wounded. "I'm ready to assist in any way I can."

Brandon, eager to contribute, added, "I'll do whatever it takes, sir."

Colonel Stevens nodded, his expression softening slightly. "Your dedication is commendable. We'll get through this together. Now, let's get to work."

Chapter 5

"Welcome," he said, his voice deep and resonant. "You must be the new recruits. I'm Sergeant Johnson, in charge of this little outfit. You two have been assigned to our medical unit. Hilary, I believe you're our new medic, and Brandon, you'll be part of the support squad."

Hilary stepped forward, her eyes bright with determination. "I'm ready to help in any way I can. As a nurse, and I'll do whatever it takes to aid our soldiers and civilians."

Sergeant Johnson nodded approvingly. "That's the spirit we need around here. You'll be a valuable asset, no doubt."

"Thank you, sir." Brandon replied.

Sergeant Johnson nodded. "Here are your uniforms," he added, handing the duo military fatigues and combat boots. "You can we changed and once you are dressed I can take you to your barracks."

Brandon and Hilary nodded and went inside the changing rooms nearby. Once dressed they exited the rooms, and they stood dressed in standard military tan camouflage uniforms. Standing in the crisp outfit, Brandon grinned. He looked over at Hillary and smiled.

"You look great, Hilary." He complimented.

"You do too. I love a man in uniform." Hilary flirted.

Brandon blushed and looked down at his boots.

Sergeant Johnson cleared his throat breaking the romantic tension that filled the air. "Now, let's get you settled in. We have a civilian barrack where you'll be staying. It's not much, but it provides some shelter and a place to rest."

They followed the sergeant through the camp, passing rows of tents and makeshift shelters. The area buzzed with activity as people cooked meals, cleaned weapons, and shared stories of the day's battles. Finally, they reached a large tent with a sign that read "Civilian Barrack C." Inside, a dozen cots were lined up, most already occupied by weary men and women.

"This is it," Sergeant Johnson announced. "There's one cot left, and unfortunately, we're a bit tight on space. One of you will have to make do with sleeping outside or sharing cots. I know it's not ideal, but we're doing the best we can."

Hilary scanned the room, her heart sinking as she realized the situation. "Brandon, there's only one bed," she whispered, her voice filled with concern. "You should take it. You're the only person I know here, and I'd feel better knowing you're safe and comfortable."

Brandon shook his head, his eyes fixed on her with unwavering determination. "No, you take it, Hilary. You've been through so much already, and you need your rest. I'll be fine sleeping outside. Besides, we can take turns if we need to."

Hilary's eyes widened at his selflessness. "I can't let you do that. I mean, look at this place. It's a mess. I can't leave you out there."

"It's okay," Brandon reassured her, placing a gentle hand on her shoulder. "I'll be fine. We're in this together, remember? And who knows, maybe I'll get lucky and find a spare cot somewhere."

As they debated, an older woman with graying hair spoke up from her cot. "You two seem close. Why don't you just share the bed? There's plenty of room for two."

Hilary's cheeks flushed, and Brandon's eyes widened in surprise. They exchanged a glance, a mix of embarrassment and amusement.

"Well, I guess that's one solution," Brandon said, grinning. "But we can't just..."

"No, it's fine," Hilary interrupted, her voice softening. "We're both adults, and it's not like we haven't... you know..." She trailed off, her eyes darting to the floor.

The other occupants of the barrack chuckled, some nodding in agreement. Sergeant Johnson cleared his throat, a hint of amusement in his eyes. "Alright, you two can work it out between yourselves. Just make sure you get some rest. We'll need you both at your best tomorrow."

As the sergeant left, Hilary and Brandon found themselves alone in the crowded barrack. They stood awkwardly for a moment, unsure of what to do next. Finally, Brandon spoke, his voice quiet and sincere.

"Look, Hilary, I know this is a crazy situation. I want you to know that I'm here for you, no matter what. We can share the bed, or we can take turns. Whatever makes you feel comfortable."

Hilary's eyes welled up with emotion. "Brandon, you've been incredible. I can't believe I only met you last night. It feels like I've known you forever. I don't want you to be uncomfortable or feel obliged to do this."

"I'm not doing it out of obligation," he said, taking her hands in his. "I want to be with you. I want to protect you, and I'll do whatever it takes to make sure you're safe. Even if it means sleeping on the ground."

Hilary's heart raced as she looked into Brandon's eyes. She could see the sincerity and concern etched on his face. "I don't want you to be uncomfortable because of me," she said softly. "I'll sleep on the floor if that's what you prefer."

Brandon shook his head, a smile playing on his lips. "No, that's not what I want. I want to be with you, Hilary. I trust you, and I know you trust me. Let's share the bed, and we can figure out the rest as we go."

Hilary's resistance melted away, and she found herself nodding in agreement. "Okay, we'll share the bed. But I want to make it clear that I'm doing this because I want to, not because I feel pressured."

"I understand," Brandon said, squeezing her hands gently. "I respect your decision, and I'm honored that you trust me enough to share this space with me."

As they settled into the cot, Brandon's eyes sparkled with mischief. "So, here we are, sharing a bed in the middle of a war-zone. Who would've thought our night at the club would lead to this?"

Hilary laughed, the sound filling the small space. "I certainly didn't. I mean, I never expected to find myself in the middle of an invasion, let alone sharing a bed with a man I just met."

"Well, it's a crazy world," Brandon said, his voice low and husky. "And I'm glad I met you, Hilary. You're an incredible woman, and I'm grateful to have you by my side."

Hilary's heart fluttered as she felt his gaze on her. "You're pretty incredible yourself, Brandon. I never thought I'd find someone who would make me feel so safe and cared for, especially in these circumstances."

Their eyes locked, and the tension between them grew palpable. Brandon leaned in, his breath warm against her skin. "I want to take care of you, Hilary. I want to protect you and make sure you're okay. I don't want to push you, but I can't deny that I want you."

Hilary's breath caught in her throat as she felt his desire. "I want you too, Brandon. I mean, I've never felt this way before. It's like we're connected, even though we barely know each other."

As if on cue, the sound of distant explosions rumbled through the night, reminding them of the danger lurking beyond the safety of the barrack. Brandon pulled her closer, his arms wrapping around her protectively. "We'll face this together, Hilary. I won't let anything happen to you. I promise."

Hilary snuggled into his embrace, feeling a sense of peace amidst the chaos. "I know, Brandon. I trust you. And I'm glad we have each other in this crazy situation."

As they held each other, their fears and desires intertwined, the world outside seemed to fade away. The sound of gunfire and explosions became a distant backdrop to their intimate moment. Brandon's lips found Hilary's, and they kissed passionately, their bodies yearning for comfort and connection.

The kiss deepened, and Brandon's hands roamed over her curves, igniting a fire within her. Hilary responded eagerly, her hands exploring his strong body. Their passion grew, fueled by the uncertainty of their future and the intensity of their newfound bond.

As their embrace became more urgent, Brandon's hand slipped beneath her shirt, caressing her soft skin. Hilary arched into his touch, her breath coming in short gasps. Their kisses became more fervent, and they lost themselves in the moment, forgetting the war and the world around them.

Just as their passion threatened to consume them, the sound of footsteps and voices outside the barrack snapped them back to reality, and the duo remembered they weren't alone. Hilary and Brandon, breathless and flushed, broke apart, their hearts pounding.

"We should probably get some sleep," Brandon whispered, his voice hoarse with desire. "We have a long day ahead of us tomorrow."

Hilary nodded, her eyes sparkling with unspoken promises. "Yes, we should rest. But Brandon..." She paused, her fingers tracing his jawline. "I want you to know that I'm looking forward to waking up next to you."

Brandon's heart swelled with joy and desire. "I can't wait to wake up with you, Hilary. I have a feeling tomorrow will be a whole new adventure."

As they settled into the cot, their bodies intertwined, the outside world seemed to disappear. The chaos of the invasion, the fear, and the uncertainty faded away, leaving only the warmth of their embrace and the promise of a new day.

Little did they know, the battle for Virginia Beach was far from over, and their role in it was about to become even more crucial. But for now, in each other's arms, they found solace and strength, ready to face whatever challenges the war would bring.

Chapter 6

As the sun rose over Virginia Beach, casting a soft golden hue across the war-torn city, Brandon and Hilary woke up in each other's arms, their temporary sanctuary amidst the chaos. The previous night's passion had deepened their connection, and now they faced the harsh reality of war together. With the sounds of distant gunfire and explosions echoing in the background, they prepared for their first mission, knowing that their actions could make a significant difference in the battle for their beloved city.

Brandon, still feeling the weight of responsibility on his broad shoulders, rose from the makeshift bed, his brown eyes filled with determination. He had never imagined himself in such a situation, but the events of the past few days had pushed him to discover an inner strength he didn't know he possessed. He was no longer just an accountant with dreams of becoming a millionaire; he was a fighter, a protector, and a vital part of the resistance.

Hilary, her curvy figure wrapped in a blanket, sat up and stretched, her brown hair falling gracefully around her shoulders. She had always been the life of the party, a witty and outgoing nurse who loved to care for others. But now, her skills were needed in a different way, and she was ready to step up and make a difference. The thought of helping her fellow citizens and fighting for her home gave her a newfound sense of purpose.

"We've got a big day ahead of us," Brandon said, his voice soft yet resolute. "The militia is planning a counterattack, and we're going to play a crucial role."

Hilary's eyes sparkled with a mixture of excitement and apprehension. "We're really doing this, aren't we? I never imagined I'd be part of something like this, but I'm ready. I want to help in any way I can."

They shared a brief moment of silence, reflecting on the gravity of the situation. The previous night, they had found comfort in each other's embrace, but the war showed no mercy, and they knew the price of freedom was high.

The militia camp bustled with activity as soldiers prepared for the upcoming mission. Sergeant Johnson, a seasoned veteran with a weathered face, gathered the group, including Brandon and Hilary, for a briefing.

"Listen up, folks!" Sergeant Johnson's voice boomed, cutting through the morning air. "We've got intelligence that the Russians have set up a warehouse on the outskirts of the city, stockpiling food and supplies. These resources are crucial for their war effort, and we aim to take it back. This mission is vital, but it won't be easy. We expect heavy resistance, so stay sharp and follow orders. We leave at 0400, and will use the cover of the night and early morning to our advantage."

Brandon and Hilary exchanged nervous glances, understanding the magnitude of the task. Capturing the warehouse would be a significant blow to the enemy, but it would come at a cost.

As the group geared up, Brandon approached Hilary, his eyes filled with concern. "Are you sure you're ready for this? It's going to be dangerous, and I don't want you to feel pressured into doing something you're not comfortable with."

Hilary placed her hand on Brandon's cheek, her touch gentle and reassuring. "I'm ready, Brandon. I chose to stay and fight, and I believe in what we're doing. Besides, we're in this together, remember?"

He smiled, his heart warmed by her unwavering support. "Together, always," he whispered, leaning in to kiss her softly.

The next day the militia set out under the cover of dawn, moving stealthily through the streets of Virginia Beach. Brandon and Hilary were assigned to a small team tasked with providing medical support and gathering intelligence. They navigated the city's ruins, their hearts pounding with anticipation and fear. The once vibrant streets were now a haunting reminder of the war's devastation. Hilary and Brandon were both dressed in their standard military fatigues, along with body armor, helmets and rifles.

As they approached the warehouse, the team split into two groups. Brandon and Hilary followed Sergeant Johnson and a few others to the rear entrance, while the remaining soldiers moved to the front. The plan was to attack from both sides, catching the Russians off guard.

"Remember, stay low and move quickly," Sergeant Johnson instructed. "We'll provide covering fire, but the element of surprise is key. Hilary, you and Brandon will be right behind us, ready to tend to any injuries."

They nodded, their eyes scanning the surroundings for any signs of enemy movement. The warehouse, a large concrete structure, loomed ahead, its walls pockmarked with bullet holes.

With a hand signal from Sergeant Johnson, the team sprang into action. They rushed towards the entrance, guns blazing, taking cover behind abandoned vehicles and crates. Brandon and Hilary hugged the ground, their hearts racing as bullets whizzed overhead. The sound of gunfire and explosions filled the air, a deafening symphony of war.

"Stay down!" Brandon shouted to Hilary as he pulled her closer to the cover of a large container. "We'll move when it's safe."

Hilary, her face smeared with dirt and sweat, nodded, her hands steady as she prepared her medical kit. "I'm ready to help, Brandon. Just give the word."

The initial assault was fierce, and the Russians were caught off guard. The American soldiers fought with determination, pushing their way into the warehouse. Brandon and Hilary crawled forward, tending to wounded comrades along the way. The warehouse interior was a maze of stacked supplies, providing ample cover for both sides.

As they moved deeper, the fighting intensified. Brandon, his heart pounding, helped a wounded soldier to safety, dodging enemy fire. Hilary, with swift and precise movements, administered first aid, her nursing skills saving lives on the battlefield.

The Russians, realizing their position was compromised, began to retreat, but not before setting up a final line of defense. The American soldiers pressed forward, determined to secure the warehouse. Brandon and Hilary found themselves in the thick of the battle, taking cover behind a stack of crates.

"We're almost there," Brandon shouted over the deafening gunfire. "Just a little further, and we'll have the warehouse!"

Hilary, her eyes focused on a wounded soldier nearby, nodded, her hands moving swiftly to stop the bleeding. "I won't let anyone down," she said, her voice steady despite the chaos.

In a final push, the American soldiers overwhelmed the remaining Russian defenders. The warehouse was secured, but the cost was high. Brandon and Hilary emerged from their cover, their eyes taking in the grim scene. Soldiers, both friend and foe, lay wounded or dead, a stark reminder of the war's brutality.

Hilary rushed to tend to the injured, her medical kit in hand. Brandon, overcome with emotion, surveyed the warehouse, now under American control. The shelves were lined with food and supplies, a crucial victory for the city's survival.

"We did it," Brandon said, his voice hoarse with emotion. "We captured the warehouse, but at what cost?"

Hilary, her hands stained with blood, looked up at Brandon, her eyes filled with determination. "We did what we had to do, Brandon. This is the reality of war. We'll honor the fallen by using these supplies to help our people."

As the sun climbed higher in the sky, the surviving soldiers began the arduous task of securing the warehouse and tending to the wounded. Brandon and Hilary worked tirelessly, their bond strengthened by the shared trauma and the knowledge that their actions had made a difference.

The battle for Virginia Beach was far from over, but the victory at the warehouse provided a glimmer of hope. Brandon and Hilary, once strangers thrown together by fate, had become an integral part of the resistance, their love and determination fueling their fight for freedom.

Chapter 7

Brandon Hill and Hilary Tork, their hearts still pounding from the adrenaline of battle, found themselves in a rare moment of tranquility amidst the chaos. They had been assigned to defend the newly captured warehouse, a strategic stronghold in their fight against the Russian invaders. But for now, the warehouse was quiet, almost eerily so, providing them with a brief respite from the relentless war.

Brandon and Hilary, their eyes locking across the dimly lit room, shared a silent understanding. The stress of the past few days had forged a deep connection between them, and their feelings for each other had grown stronger with each shared experience. They were more than just comrades-in-arms; they were a lifeline to each other in this war-torn world.

"We finally have a moment to ourselves," Brandon whispered, his voice soft and full of emotion. His dark eyes glistened with a mixture of desire and relief as he took in the sight of Hilary, standing before him in her worn combat gear, her brown hair slightly disheveled, but her face radiant with determination.

Hilary smiled, her blue eyes sparkling with mischief. "I can't believe we're here, alive and together. It feels like we've been running and fighting non-stop." She took a step towards him, her movements graceful despite the heavy boots she wore.

Brandon nodded, his heart racing as he realized the opportunity that had presented itself. "I've been wanting this moment since the first time we met. Just you and me, without the chaos of war breathing down our necks." He took her hands in his, his slender fingers entwining with hers.

"I want to show you how much you mean to me, Hilary. How much I care."

As Brandon spoke, Hilary's breath quickened, and her cheeks flushed with desire. She had felt a strong attraction to Brandon from the start, drawn to his intelligence, courage, and gentle nature. In a world that had turned upside down, he had become her rock, her source of comfort and strength.

"I want that too, Brandon," she replied, her voice husky with emotion. "I've never felt this way before. You make me feel safe, even in the midst of all this madness." She leaned in, her lips brushing his gently. "I want to be with you, here and now. Just us."

Brandon's eyes widened with surprise and delight as Hilary's lips touched his. He had dreamed of this moment, but the reality of it was even more intense. He kissed her back, his lips parting slightly, inviting her in. Their tongues met in a slow, sensual dance, exploring each other with a hunger that had been building for days.

Pulling her closer, Brandon wrapped his arms around Hilary's waist, his hands sliding up her back, caressing her through her clothing. He could feel her curves pressing against him, her soft breasts molding into his chest, her hips caving into his groin. The sensation was electrifying, and he groaned softly into her mouth, his body responding to her touch.

Hilary moaned in response, her hands sliding up Brandon's back, under his shirt, her fingers tracing the muscles of his bulky frame. She loved the feel of his warm skin against her palms, the contrast of his soft flesh and the hard planes of his body. Brandon was stout and strong, and she delighted in the way he made her feel so protected and desired at the same time.

Breaking the kiss, Brandon trailed his lips down Hilary's neck, leaving a trail of wet kisses that made her shiver with pleasure. He found the sensitive spot just below her ear and nibbled gently, causing her to gasp and clutch at his shoulders.

"Brandon, please," she whispered, her voice breathless. "I need you."

He looked up, his brown eyes dark with desire. "I need you too, Hilary. I want to make you feel good, to show you how much I care."

With that, Brandon lifted Hilary into his arms, making her giggle as he carried her across the room. They had scouted the warehouse earlier, ensuring it was safe and finding an empty office space that offered some privacy. Now, Brandon laid Hilary gently on a large wooden desk, the cool surface contrasting with the heat between them.

Hilary watched Brandon through half-lidded eyes as he undressed, his movements graceful and confident. His muscular body was a work of art, and she couldn't help but admire the way his dark skin gleamed in the soft light. Brandon's manhood, already semi-erect, stood proudly, a testament to his desire for her.

"You're so beautiful," she whispered, reaching out to stroke his length gently.

Brandon groaned at her touch, his eyes closing momentarily as he savored the sensation. "I'm all yours, Hilary. Take what you want."

Hilary's heart raced as she explored Brandon's body, her fingers tracing the contours of his chest, his nipples hardening under her touch. She leaned up to kiss his neck, her lips moving down his chest, tasting the saltiness of his skin. Her hands continued their exploration, sliding down his hips, cupping his firm buttocks, and squeezing gently.

"You feel so good," she murmured, her breath hot against his skin.

Brandon's control was slipping, his need for her overwhelming. He wanted to pleasure her, to make her feel the same intensity he was experiencing. With a swift motion, he unfastened Hilary's pants, sliding them down her legs, revealing her lace panties and the smooth curves of her pale thighs.

"So beautiful," he whispered, his voice hoarse with desire.

Hilary's breath caught as Brandon's lips found the sensitive skin of her inner thighs, his kisses sending shivers through her body. He gently nudged her legs apart, his fingers hooking into the waistband of her panties, slowly sliding them down her legs.

"Oh, Brandon," she moaned, her back arching off the desk as his warm breath caressed her most intimate place.

Brandon's mouth replaced his fingers, his tongue parting her wet folds, tasting her sweetness. He teased her clit with gentle strokes, his hands holding her hips, feeling her tremble with pleasure. Hilary's hands threaded through his hair, guiding him, urging him on as he continued to pleasure her with his skilled mouth.

"I'm close," she whispered, her voice strained. "Oh God, Brandon, don't stop."

Brandon smiled against her, his tongue flicking faster, driving her to the edge. Hilary's body tensed, her back arching, and she cried out his name as her orgasm crashed over her. He continued to lap at her, riding out her waves of pleasure, until she collapsed back onto the desk, her body trembling.

Brandon lifted his head, his face glistening with her essence, and smiled at her. "You're amazing, Hilary. I love the way you taste."

Hilary, still breathing heavily, reached for him, pulling him up for a deep, passionate kiss. "I want you inside me, Brandon. Please."

He needed no further encouragement. Brandon positioned himself between her legs, his manhood throbbing with anticipation. He entered her slowly, filling her inch by inch, his eyes never leaving hers. Hilary's walls clenched around him, hot and wet, and he groaned, his control slipping further.

"You feel incredible," he whispered, his voice thick with desire.

She nodded, her eyes heavy-lidded with pleasure. "More, Brandon. Please, more."

Brandon began to move, his hips thrusting in a slow, steady rhythm. Each stroke sent waves of pleasure through Hilary's body, and she matched his pace, her nails digging into his back, leaving marks of passion. Their movements became more urgent, their bodies slick with sweat, as they found a rhythm that pushed them both towards the edge.

"Brandon, I'm close," Hilary gasped, her voice hoarse. "I want to come with you."

He nodded, his breath coming in short pants. "Together, Hilary. I want to feel you come around me."

Their pace quickened, their bodies moving as one, driven by a primal need. Brandon's thrusts became more intense, his hips slamming into hers, and Hilary cried out, her release shattering through her. Brandon followed, his body convulsing as he emptied himself into her, their cries of pleasure echoing in the empty office.

In the aftermath of their passion, Brandon and Hilary lay entangled on the desk, their hearts still racing. Brandon brushed the hair from Hilary's face, his thumb tracing her lips.

"I'm so happy that I'm with you, Hilary," he whispered, his voice filled with emotion.

Hilary's eyes filled with tears of joy as she smiled up at him. "I am happy too, Brandon. I never thought I'd find someone like you in the middle of all this chaos."

"I know the whole boyfriend and girlfriend thing doesn't really matter in a war zone but..."

"Yes, I want to. I want to be your girlfriend."

"Really?"

"Oh course, you're more of a man than any of my prior boyfriends combined."

"And you could kick the ass of any of my exs." Brandon joked.

They both laughed and then kissed each other once more, their lips moving together in a slow, tender dance, their love and passion deepening with each touch. But their moment of peace was fleeting, as the sounds of war began to filter back into their consciousness.

"We should get back to the others," Hilary said reluctantly, sitting up and reaching for her clothes. "They'll be wondering where we are."

Brandon nodded, a slight sadness creeping into his eyes. "I know. But we have each other now, and we'll face whatever comes together."

As they dressed, the reality of their situation began to sink in. They had just shared an incredibly intimate moment, declaring their love for each other in the midst of a war zone. But the battle for Virginia Beach was far from over, and they had a crucial role to play in its defense.

Hand in hand, Brandon and Hilary left the office, their connection stronger than ever. They knew the challenges ahead would be immense, but they faced them with renewed determination, their love a beacon of hope in the darkness of war.

As they rejoined the other fighters, preparing for the next assault, Brandon and Hilary exchanged a secret smile, knowing that no matter what the future held, they would face it together, their love a powerful force in the midst of the chaos.

Chapter 8

As the sun rose over Virginia Beach, casting a pale orange hue across the sky, Brandon and Hilary awoke in each other's arms, their bodies entangled on the makeshift bed in the corner of the captured warehouse. The previous night's events had brought them closer, and their love had blossomed amidst the chaos of war. They had found solace in one another, a sanctuary in the midst of destruction.

Brandon, his muscular frame relaxed after a restful night, gently brushed the brown locks away from Hilary's face, his fingers tracing the curve of her cheek. Hilary, her curvy figure snuggled against Brandon's warmth, smiled sleepily, her brown eyes sparkling with affection. "Good morning, handsome," she whispered, her voice soft from sleep. Brandon leaned in, his lips brushing against hers in a tender kiss, their love language, a quiet moment in the storm of war.

Waking up in the warehouse was becoming a regular thing for them, something they never imagined. However, this morning was different. The sounds of the city were not the usual hum of activity and distant gunfire. Instead, a deep silence filled the air, an eerie calm before the storm. Brandon's instincts, honed by the recent battles, immediately went on high alert.

"Something's not right," he murmured, his soft-spoken nature belying the intensity in his brown eyes. Hilary, her outgoing spirit momentarily subdued by Brandon's concern, nodded in agreement. "I have a bad feeling about this. It's too quiet."

They quickly dressed and got prepared to leave on patrol. As they stepped out of the warehouse, the morning light revealed a haunting sight. The once bustling city streets were now deserted, devoid of life.

The only movement came from a distant plume of smoke rising into the sky, a grim reminder of the ongoing conflict. While patrolling the perimeter of the warehouse something felt off, and the duo couldn't place their finger on it.

"We should find the others," Hilary suggested, her voice steady despite the unsettling atmosphere. Brandon nodded, his gaze scanning the area for any signs of their fellow militia members. "Let's head back towards the warehouse. We can regroup there."

They moved swiftly, their footsteps echoing off the empty buildings. The silence was unnerving, as if the city was holding its breath, waiting for an impending catastrophe. As they turned a corner, a loud explosion shattered the stillness, sending shockwaves through the air. Brandon and Hilary were thrown to the ground, their ears ringing from the blast.

"What the—!" Brandon exclaimed, his voice drowned out by the thunderous noise. Hilary scrambled to her feet, her nurse's training kicking in as she assessed Brandon for injuries. "Are you okay? Any broken bones?" she asked, her eyes searching for signs of trauma.

Brandon, dazed but unharmed, shook his head and helped Hilary up. "I'm fine, but that explosion came from the warehouse we just left." They exchanged worried glances, knowing that their comrades were still inside. Without a word, they sprinted back, their hearts pounding with fear and determination.

The once sturdy warehouse was now a burning inferno, flames licking the sky, and smoke billowing out, obscuring the sun. The Americans were in disarray, some running for cover, while others bravely fought back against the Russian assault. Brandon and Hilary witnessed the horror as their friends and fellow militia members fell, caught in the crossfire.

"We have to help!" Hilary cried, her nurse's instinct compelling her to rush towards the wounded. Brandon, his accountant's mind quickly assessing the situation, grabbed her hand. "It's too dangerous. We need to fall back. The Russians have us outgunned." Brandon noted watching Russians gun down all their militia members.

Reluctantly, Hilary nodded, tears welling up in her eyes as she witnessed the devastating scene. They turned to retreat, but a second explosion, closer this time, sent them tumbling to the ground. When the smoke cleared, they realized they were alone, separated from their unit, and surrounded by enemy forces.

"We're behind enemy lines," Brandon whispered, his voice barely audible over the chaos. Hilary's eyes widened with fear, but her determination remained unwavering. "We have to find a way out. We can't stay here."

They crawled behind a toppled pillar, seeking cover from the relentless gunfire. Brandon, his intelligence and strategic thinking coming to the fore, peered cautiously around the corner, assessing their options. "We can't go back the way we came. The Russians have set up a blockade. We need to find an alternate route."

Hilary, her life-of-the-party demeanor replaced by a steely resolve, nodded in agreement. "We'll have to go through the old factory district. It's risky, but it might be our only chance."

With a shared look of understanding, they set off, navigating the maze of abandoned buildings and debris-filled streets. The sounds of battle gradually faded, but the tension remained palpable as they knew the Russians could be lurking around any corner.

As they reached the outskirts of the factory district, Brandon spotted a group of Russian soldiers on patrol, their weapons slung casually over their shoulders. "Down!" he hissed, pulling Hilary into a crouch behind a rusted car.

"We can't let them see us," Brandon whispered, his heart pounding. "We'll have to make our way through the factories without being noticed."

Hilary's eyes darted around, searching for a solution. "I have an idea. We can use the smoke from the burning warehouse to our advantage. It will provide some cover."

Brandon nodded, impressed by her quick thinking. They waited patiently, their hearts racing, as the patrol passed by, their footsteps echoing off the concrete. As soon as the coast was clear, they sprinted towards the nearest factory entrance, their movements swift and stealthy.

Inside the dimly lit factory, the air was thick with dust and the acrid smell of burning rubber. Hilary coughed, covering her mouth with her sleeve, as they made their way through the labyrinth of machinery and conveyor belts.

"This place is huge," Hilary whispered, her voice echoing off the metal surfaces. "We need to find a way out without getting lost."

Brandon, his soft-spoken nature now a source of calm, pointed to a faint light at the end of the factory floor. "Let's head towards that. It might lead to an exit."

They crept forward, their footsteps silent on the grimy floor. As they approached the light, they discovered a small office with a broken window, offering a glimpse of the outside world.

"Thank goodness," Hilary breathed, her relief evident. "We can climb out and make our way back to the militia camp."

As they prepared to exit, a loud crash startled them. Brandon spun around, his eyes widening at the sight of a Russian soldier standing in the doorway, his weapon raised. Hilary, acting on instinct, grabbed a nearby wrench and hurled it at the soldier, catching him off guard. The soldier stumbled, giving Brandon enough time to charge forward and tackle him to the ground.

They grappled, Brandon's muscular frame pitted against the soldier's military training. Hilary, not one to stand idly by, grabbed a fire extinguisher and smashed it across the soldier's head, knocking him unconscious.

"Nice work, baby," Brandon panted, a mix of adrenaline and relief coursing through him. Hilary, her hands trembling, smiled at Brandon, their shared experience forging an even stronger bond between them.

"We make a pretty good team, don't we, babe?" she said, her voice shaking slightly. Brandon nodded, his brown eyes filled with admiration. "We do. And we're not done yet. We have to get back to the camp and warn them about the Russian advance."

With renewed determination, they climbed out of the factory, their hearts heavy with the knowledge of the losses suffered by their friends. The journey back to the militia camp was a silent one, each lost in their thoughts, reflecting on the horrors they had witnessed and the strength they had found in each other.

As they approached the camp, the sight that greeted them was one of chaos and desperation. The American forces, depleted and battered, were preparing for a last stand against the advancing Russians. Brandon and Hilary exchanged a worried glance, knowing their return would bring little comfort to their comrades.

"We have to do something," Hilary said, her voice filled with determination. "We can't just stand by and watch our city fall."

Brandon, his accountant's mind already processing the possibilities, had an idea. "I have a plan. It's risky, but it might buy us some time."

As the Russian forces drew closer, Brandon and Hilary, their love and courage fueling their actions, prepared to make a stand, determined to protect their city and each other, no matter the cost. The battle for Virginia Beach was far from over, and their story, a testament to the power of ordinary people in the face of extraordinary circumstances, was about to take another dramatic turn.

The fate of Virginia Beach hung in the balance, and Brandon and Hilary, an unlikely duo turned lovers and warriors, were ready to face the challenges ahead, together.

Chapter 9

Brandon stood before his commanding officer, Sergeant Johnson, his heart pounding with determination. Brandon had made up his mind; he wanted to take the fight to the Russians and reclaim the territory they had lost. It was a daring and risky proposition, but Brandon was ready to step up and lead the charge. He believed that this mission could turn the tide of the war and bring some sense of normalcy back to their beloved city.

"Sir, I want to lead a team to retake the eastern district," Brandon stated firmly, his voice steady and confident. "We can't let the Russians hold that ground any longer. It's a strategic location, and if we can drive them out, it will be a significant victory for us."

Sergeant Johnson, studied Brandon carefully. He knew the young man had proven himself in battle, but this was a different kind of challenge. Leading a mission required more than just bravery; it demanded strategic thinking and a level head. However, the Sergeant also knew that sometimes, the boldest plans were the ones that brought success.

"Son, this is a dangerous operation. The Russians have fortified their positions, and we've lost good men trying to breach their defenses. Are you sure you want to take on this responsibility?" The Sergeant's words were cautious, but there was a hint of admiration in his eyes.

Brandon stood tall, his broad shoulders squared. "I understand the risks, sir. But we can't afford to sit back and let them gain more ground. We need to strike back, and I believe I can lead a successful mission. I've studied the maps, and I have a plan."

Johnson nodded, impressed by Brandon's resolve. "Very well, Hill. You've shown exceptional leadership potential. I'll grant you command of a squad. Choose your team wisely, and make sure they're ready for what lies ahead."

Brandon's heart swelled with pride and a sense of duty. He had never imagined himself in such a position, but the war had changed him. No longer was he just an accountant with dreams of becoming a millionaire. Now, he was a warrior, fighting for his city and the woman he loved.

As Brandon prepared to leave the command tent, he spotted Hilary, her vibrant energy radiating through the camp. She had been a constant source of support and inspiration since they first met. Their relationship had blossomed amidst the chaos of war, and Brandon knew he couldn't bear the thought of losing her.

"Hey, Hil," Brandon called out, his voice softening as he approached her. "I wanted to let you know that I'm leading a mission to retake the eastern district. It's going to be dangerous, and I need you to stay here at the camp."

Hilary's eyes widened, and her lips formed a determined line. She had become an integral part of the medical unit, tending to the wounded with skill and compassion. Her bravery in the face of enemy fire had earned her the respect of the entire camp.

"No way, Brandon," she replied, her voice steady. "I'm coming with you. I can't just sit here while you're out there risking your life. Besides, someone needs to keep an eye on you." She flashed him a playful smile, but her eyes betrayed the worry she felt.

Brandon shook his head, his expression turning serious. "It's too risky, Hil. The Russians have heavy artillery in that area. We'll be outgunned, and the odds are stacked against us. I can't guarantee your safety."

"I know the risks," she insisted, stepping closer to him. "But we've faced danger together before, and we're still here. We're a team, Brandon. We fight together, we win together."

Brandon's resolve wavered as he looked into her determined eyes. He knew she was right; they had faced countless challenges as a team, and their bond had grown stronger with each trial. But the thought of losing her was unbearable.

"Listen, Hil, I can't lose you. You're everything to me. I love you, and the thought of something happening to you..." His voice trailed off, his emotions getting the better of him.

Hilary's expression softened, and she reached up to cup his cheek with her hand. "I love you too, Brandon. Meeting you at the club was the best thing that ever happened to me. But I can't just sit here while you're out there. We're in this war together, and I won't let you face it alone."

Brandon's heart ached at her words, and he pulled her into a tight embrace. He breathed in the scent of her hair, feeling her warmth against him. "Okay, we'll go together," he whispered, his voice croaked with emotion. "But promise me you'll stay close and follow my lead."

Hilary nodded, her tears dampening his shirt. "I promise. We'll face whatever comes our way, together."

As they parted, Brandon knew that their love had become a force to be reckoned with. It was a powerful motivator, driving them to protect their city and each other. He believed that their shared determination would be their greatest weapon in the battles to come.

Brandon gathered his squad, a hand-picked group of skilled fighters, and briefed them on the mission. They studied maps and devised a strategy to approach the Russian stronghold from an unexpected direction, using the cover of night to their advantage. The plan was ambitious, but with Brandon's leadership and the team's skills, they had a fighting chance.

As dusk fell, Brandon and Hilary, along with their squad, set out on their perilous journey. They moved through the city's ruins, avoiding enemy patrols and using their knowledge of the terrain to their advantage. The moon cast an eerie glow, providing just enough light to navigate the treacherous path.

The eastern district loomed ahead, a ghostly silhouette against the night sky. The Russians had set up machine gun nests and artillery positions, making it a formidable challenge. Brandon's squad took cover behind abandoned buildings, preparing for the assault.

"Remember, we hit them hard and fast," Brandon whispered to his team. "We'll use flash-bangs to disorient them, and then we move in. Stay sharp, and let's show them what Virginia Beach is made of."

Hilary, her eyes gleaming with determination, positioned herself beside Brandon. She had a med kit strapped to her waist, ready to provide medical aid if needed. Their fingers intertwined, a silent promise to each other.

With a signal from Brandon, the squad surged forward, throwing flash-bangs that exploded with blinding light and deafening noise. The Russians, caught off guard, were momentarily stunned, giving Brandon's team the crucial advantage they needed.

The squad opened fire, their weapons roaring in the night. Brandon and Hilary moved swiftly, taking cover behind a crumbled wall. They fired at the enemy positions, their aim true. The Russians returned fire, but the element of surprise had shifted the odds in Brandon's favor.

As the battle raged, Brandon's squad pushed forward, capturing one enemy position after another. Hilary tended to the wounded, her nursing skills saving lives on the battlefield. The fighting was intense, but the squad's morale remained high, fueled by Brandon's leadership and the knowledge that they were fighting for their home.

Finally, after what felt like an eternity, the Russian resistance began to falter. Brandon's squad had dealt a devastating blow, and the enemy was forced to retreat. The eastern district was back under American control, and the squad celebrated their hard-fought victory.

Brandon and Hilary, their hearts pounding with adrenaline and relief, embraced amidst the chaos. Their love had endured the trials of war, and they knew that their bond was unbreakable.

As the sun rose over the liberated district, Brandon and Hilary stood together, surveying the damage. The war was far from over, but their actions had made a difference. They had reclaimed a piece of their city, and their love had become a symbol of hope amidst the destruction.

"We did it, Hil," Brandon said, his voice filled with pride. "We showed them what we're capable of. This is just the beginning. We'll keep fighting, keep pushing back the Russians, until Virginia Beach is free."

Hilary smiled, her eyes sparkling with determination. "Together, we can do anything. This city is our home, and we won't let anyone take it from us. We'll keep fighting, Brandon, side by side, until the war is won."

Their love story, woven into the fabric of the war, had become a powerful force, inspiring those around them. As they prepared for the next challenge, they knew that their bond would continue to grow stronger, even in the shadows of war.

The battle for Virginia Beach raged on, but Brandon and Hilary's love was a beacon of light, guiding them through the darkness. Together, they would face the unknown, determined to protect their city and each other, no matter the cost.

Chapter 10

The eastern district of Virginia Beach had finally been wrested from Russian control thanks to the valiant efforts of Brandon Hill and his squad. The once-bustling streets now echoed with the sound of victory, as the citizens slowly emerged from their hiding places, their eyes filled with both relief and hope. Among the squad, the sense of accomplishment was palpable, but the battle-weary soldiers knew their work wasn't done yet. The enemy still held several key locations, and there were rumors of a prisoner camp on the outskirts of the city, where innocent civilians were being held captive.

Hilary, her medical kit slung over her shoulder, approached Brandon as he surveyed the liberated area, his muscular frame radiating a quiet strength. "We did it, Brandon," she said, her voice filled with admiration. "We really did it."

Brandon turned to face her, his dark eyes warm with affection. "We sure did, Hil. But we're not done yet. There are still people out there who need our help."

Hilary's face lit up with determination. "You're right. We can't rest until everyone is free. What's the plan?"

Brandon explained the intelligence they had received about the prisoner camp. "It's a high-risk mission, but if we can free those prisoners, it'll be a huge blow to the Russians. We need to move fast before they relocate the camp."

Hilary's heart raced at the thought of the impending operation. She knew the risks, but the prospect of saving innocent lives, especially after the recent losses they had endured, was too important to ignore. "I'm in. Let's go get our people back."

The squad gathered, and Brandon outlined the strategy. They would approach under the cover of darkness, using the remaining flash bangs to create chaos and provide an element of surprise. Hilary's role, as always, was to provide medical support and ensure the safety of the civilians.

As they made their way through the city, the streets grew quieter, the sound of their footsteps and the occasional distant gunfire punctuating the night. Brandon and Hilary walked side by side, their hands occasionally brushing against each other, a silent reminder of their bond. The moon, a silver sliver in the sky, offered little light, and the shadows danced around them, adding to the suspense.

Upon reaching the edge of the city, they encountered a heavily fortified perimeter. The Russians had set up multiple layers of defense, making the rescue operation even more challenging. Brandon signaled for the squad to halt, and they huddled together, whispering their plan of attack.

"We'll split into two teams," Brandon whispered. "Team One, you take the left flank and create a distraction. Team Two, follow me to the main gate. We'll breach it and secure the entrance, then signal for the others to join us."

Hilary, her eyes glinting with a mixture of fear and excitement, nodded at Brandon, and they shared a moment of unspoken understanding. The squad moved into position, each member focused on their role, their breath forming clouds in the chilly night air.

Team One, led by a seasoned soldier named Marcus, crept along the perimeter, planting flash bangs at strategic points. As the last bang exploded, a blinding light and deafening boom erupted, causing chaos among the Russian guards. The squad used the distraction to rush the main gate, Brandon at the forefront, his muscular frame leading the charge.

The gate, a heavy steel barrier, was locked tight. Brandon, with a determined look, signaled for a breach charge. The squad quickly set up the explosive, and with a deafening blast, the gate flew open, sending shards of metal flying. The squad rushed in, weapons drawn, their training taking over as they cleared the area of any remaining guards.

Hilary, her heart pounding, followed close behind, her medical kit ready. As they moved deeper into the camp, the sound of terrified voices reached their ears. The prisoners, men, women, and children, were huddled together in makeshift tents, their eyes wide with fear and hope.

Brandon and Hilary shared a brief, triumphant glance before turning their attention to the task at hand. Hilary rushed to the nearest tent, her medical expertise kicking in as she assessed the situation. She quickly tended to the wounded, her gentle touch and soothing words offering comfort to the traumatized prisoners.

Brandon, meanwhile, organized the squad to secure the perimeter and escort the prisoners to safety. As the first group of civilians was led out, a young woman with tear-streaked cheeks caught Hilary's attention. She recognized her immediately—it was Sarah, her childhood friend.

"Hilary?" Sarah's voice trembled as she stood up, her eyes searching for confirmation.

Hilary's heart sank as she saw the pain and grief etched on her friend's face. She rushed over and embraced Sarah, her medical kit falling to the ground. "Oh my God, Sarah. I can't believe it's you."

Sarah sobbed into Hilary's shoulder, her body shaking. "I thought I'd never see you again. I... I lost everyone, Hil. My parents, my brothers... they're all gone."

Hilary's eyes filled with tears as she held her friend tightly. "I'm so sorry, Sarah. I'm here for you. We'll get through this together."

Brandon, witnessing the emotional reunion, approached quietly, not wanting to intrude. He placed a gentle hand on Hilary's shoulder, offering silent support. Hilary looked up at him, her eyes shining with gratitude, and he smiled, his love for her evident in his gaze.

As the squad continued to evacuate the prisoners, Hilary and Sarah shared stories of their ordeal, their voices mingling with the sounds of freedom. Brandon, ever the protector, kept a watchful eye on them, ensuring their safety.

When the last of the prisoners had been escorted out, Brandon and Hilary found a quiet moment amidst the chaos. They stood together, their backs against a tent, the night sky above them a canopy of stars.

"We did it," Hilary whispered, her voice filled with emotion. "We saved them."

Brandon pulled her close, his arms wrapping around her waist. "We did. And we'll keep doing it until this city is free. We're in this together, Hil. Always."

Hilary's eyes locked with his, her heart overflowing with love and admiration. "I love you, Brandon. I don't know what I'd do without you."

Brandon's lips curved into a tender smile, and he lowered his head, capturing her mouth in a passionate kiss. Their lips moved in perfect sync, their tongues dancing, as if their kiss was a physical manifestation of their love.

As their kiss deepened, Brandon's hands roamed over Hilary's curves, the softness of her body a stark contrast to the hardness of his muscles. He cupped her breasts, his thumbs brushing over her nipples, causing her to gasp into his mouth.

Hilary's hands were equally eager, sliding under Brandon's t-shirt, exploring the defined planes of his back and shoulders. She reveled in the feel of his warm skin, her fingers tracing the scars that spoke of his bravery.

Breaking the kiss, Brandon whispered against her lips, "Let's find a place where we can be alone. I want to show you how much I love you."

Hilary's cheeks flushed with desire, and she nodded, her heart racing. They made their way through the camp, hand in hand, their love a beacon in the darkness. Brandon's squad, understanding the need for privacy, offered them a secluded tent, away from the chaos.

Inside the tent, Brandon lit a small lantern, casting a warm glow over the interior. He turned to Hilary, his eyes burning with passion. "You are so beautiful, Hil. And so brave. I want to make you feel as amazing as you make me feel."

Hilary's breath quickened as Brandon began to undress her, his fingers deftly unbuttoning her camo jacket. He kissed her neck, his lips trailing down to her collarbone, leaving a trail of fire in their wake.

As he removed her sports bra, Brandon's eyes darkened with desire at the sight of her full breasts, the nipples already taut and begging for attention. He lowered his head, taking one nipple into his mouth, suckling gently, then teasing it with his tongue.

Hilary moaned, her hands threading through his hair, urging him on. "Brandon, please..."

He switched to the other breast, lavishing it with equal attention, his free hand sliding down to cup her sex through her pants. He could feel her heat even through the fabric, and he smiled against her skin, his breath hot on her sensitive flesh.

"I want to feel you, Hil," he murmured, his voice husky with need. "Let me take care of you."

Hilary nodded, her breath coming in short gasps as Brandon unbuttoned her camo pants and slid them down her legs. She stepped out of her clothes, standing before him in nothing but her underwear, her body trembling with anticipation.

Brandon's gaze traveled over her, taking in every inch of her beauty. He hooked his thumbs into the waistband of her panties, slowly sliding them down, revealing the dark curls between her thighs.

"You're perfect," he whispered, his voice thick with emotion. "So damn perfect."

Hilary's hands reached for his belt, eager to return the favor. She unbuckled it, her fingers brushing against the bulge in his pants, causing Brandon to groan softly. With practiced ease, she unfastened his pants and pushed them down, revealing his impressive erection, straining against his boxers.

"Oh, Brandon," she breathed, her eyes fixed on his length. "I want you so much."

Brandon stepped out of his clothes, kicking them aside, and pulled Hilary close, their bodies flush against each other. He kissed her deeply, his tongue exploring her mouth as his hands roamed over her body, reacquainting himself with every curve and hollow.

"I want to taste you," he murmured against her lips. "May I?"

Hilary's eyes widened, a mixture of surprise and desire. "Yes, please," she whispered, her voice barely audible.

Brandon gently guided her to the cot, lowering her onto the soft surface. He knelt between her legs, his eyes locked on her core, a perfect contrast of pink and brown. He leaned forward, inhaling her scent, his breath causing her to shiver.

With a gentle touch, Brandon parted her folds, revealing her glistening clit. He blew softly, sending a shiver of pleasure through Hilary's body. Then, with slow, deliberate licks, he began to taste her, his tongue exploring every inch of her sensitive flesh.

Hilary moaned, her hands gripping the cot as waves of pleasure washed over her. Brandon's mouth was a masterpiece of sensation, his tongue flicking and circling her clit, driving her wild with desire. He sucked gently, then harder, sending her spiraling towards the edge.

"Brandon, I'm close," she gasped, her hips arching off the cot.

Brandon, sensing her impending release, increased the pace, his tongue working her clit with relentless precision. Hilary's body tensed, every muscle tightening as an orgasm ripped through her, causing her to cry out his name.

Brandon continued to pleasure her through the waves of her climax, his tongue never faltering, until she collapsed back onto the cot, her body trembling. He smiled, his face glistening with her essence, and kissed her inner thigh, marking her with his possession.

"That was incredible," Hilary breathed, her eyes shining with pleasure. "I've never felt anything like that."

Brandon climbed onto the cot, his body hovering over hers, his erection pressing against her thigh. "It's just the beginning, baby. I want to make you feel even more."

Hilary's heart pounded as Brandon positioned himself at her entrance, the head of his cock nudging her wetness. With a slow, deliberate thrust, he slid into her, filling her completely.

She gasped, her body adjusting to his size, and Brandon paused, giving her a moment to savor the sensation. "You feel so good, Hil. So tight around me."

Hilary, her eyes closed in pleasure, nodded, her hands gripping his shoulders. "More, Brandon. Please, more."

Brandon began to move, his hips thrusting in a slow, steady rhythm. He withdrew almost completely before plunging back into her, each stroke eliciting a moan from Hilary's lips.

"You like that, baby?" he grunted, his voice rough with desire. "You feel so damn good."

"Yes," Hilary panted, her nails digging into his shoulders. "Harder, Brandon. Fuck me harder."

Brandon complied, his thrusts becoming more urgent, his hips slamming into hers. The cot creaked with each powerful stroke, the sound of their bodies colliding a rhythmic accompaniment to their passionate dance.

Hilary's breath came in short gasps, her body tensing with each thrust. Brandon's name was a constant refrain on her lips, her nails leaving marks on his back as she clung to him.

"I'm close," Brandon grunted, his muscles straining as he fought for control. "I want to come inside you, Hil. I want to feel you milk my cock."

Hilary's body was on fire, every nerve ending alive with sensation. "Yes, Brandon. Please, fill me up. I want to feel you come."

Brandon's control snapped, and he pounded into her, his hips a blur as he drove himself deep, over and over. Hilary's climax built, a coiling tension that exploded as Brandon filled her, his hot seed flooding her depths.

They came together, their cries of pleasure filling the tent. Brandon collapsed onto Hilary, his body trembling, his heart pounding against hers. They lay entwined, their sweat-slicked bodies glowing in the lantern's soft light.

"I love you, Hil," Brandon whispered, his lips brushing her temple. "I'll always be here for you."

Hilary smiled, her eyes shining with love. "I love you, too, Brandon. We'll get through this war together, just like we got through everything else."

As they lay there, spent and satisfied, the sounds of the camp outside faded into the background. In that moment, it was just Brandon and Hilary, two lovers finding solace and strength in each other's arms. A bond forged in the heat of battle, strengthened by their love, ready to face whatever challenges lay ahead.

Chapter 11

The sun had just begun its descent over Virginia Beach, casting a warm glow on the once vibrant city now marred by the scars of war. Brandon and Hilary, their faces smeared with dirt and sweat, made their way through the abandoned streets, the echoes of their footsteps punctuating the eerie silence. They had been assigned a crucial mission by their commanding officer—a mission that could turn the tide of the battle and bring freedom back to their beloved city.

Their orders were clear: scout and gather intelligence on a nearby Russian base. The success of this operation rested solely on their shoulders, a responsibility that weighed heavily on Brandon's mind. He had always been the quiet, analytical type, more comfortable with numbers and financial statements than with guns and warfare. But the war had changed him, and now, with Hilary by his side, he found strength in their bond.

"This place is eerily quiet," Hilary whispered, her eyes scanning the deserted streets. She was the opposite of Brandon in many ways—lively, outspoken, and always ready for adventure. Her vibrant personality was a welcome contrast to the grim surroundings. "I feel like we're the only ones left in this city."

Brandon nodded; his gaze fixed on the Russian base looming in the distance. "We need to be cautious. The CO wants us to gather intel without being detected. It's a delicate operation."

Hilary gave him a reassuring smile, her dimples deepening. "We're a great team, Brandon. We've got this. Besides, we've been through worse, remember?"

He couldn't help but smile back, recalling the numerous close calls they had survived together. Their relationship had blossomed amidst the chaos of war, forging an unbreakable connection. "Yeah, we have. And we'll get through this too."

As they approached an abandoned house, a potential vantage point for their mission, Brandon's heart raced with anticipation. The house, once a cozy home, now stood empty and desolate, its windows like hollow eyes staring back at them. They stepped inside, their boots creaking on the wooden floor.

"This place gives me the creeps," Hilary said, her voice echoing in the empty hallway. "But it's the perfect spot to observe the base without being seen."

Brandon nodded, his eyes scanning the rooms for any signs of life. "Let's split up and search for anything useful. We'll meet back here in five minutes."

They dispersed, each taking a different route through the house. Brandon's heart pounded in his chest as he moved from room to room, his senses alert for any potential danger. He found discarded military gear, evidence of the previous occupants' hasty retreat, but nothing of immediate use for their mission.

In one of the bedrooms, Brandon paused, his eyes drawn to a feminine touch in the decor. A soft pink blanket lay folded on the bed, and a half-empty bottle of perfume sat on the dresser. It was a stark reminder of the lives disrupted by the war, the families torn apart. He wondered about the woman who had once called this place home, her dreams and aspirations now shattered.

Suddenly, a soft gasp startled him, and he spun around, his hand reaching for his sidearm. There, in the doorway, stood Hilary, her eyes wide with surprise. But it wasn't fear that flashed across her face; it was a mischievous grin that sent his heart racing for a different reason.

"What's this?" Brandon asked, his voice catching in his throat.

Hilary struck a pose, her hands on her hips, and Brandon's eyes widened as he took in her appearance. She had changed out of her combat gear and into a sultry outfit—a tight black dress that hugged her curves, revealing a generous amount of cleavage. Her long, brown hair cascaded over her shoulders, and her lips were painted a seductive red. It was a stark contrast to the tough warrior he knew her to be.

"I thought we could play a little game," she purred, sauntering towards him. "You know, role-play. We can pretend we're a couple, living in this house, and I'm your sexy wife."

Brandon's mouth went dry as his mind struggled to process this unexpected turn of events. He had never imagined Hilary like this, so bold and seductive. His body responded instantly, his pulse quickening, and his dick hardening beneath his pants. "I... I don't know what to say," he stammered.

"Say yes," she whispered, her voice husky with desire. "Play along with me, Brandon. We deserve a little fun, don't we?"

He couldn't deny the heat that flared between them, the undeniable attraction that had grown stronger with each shared experience. "Okay," he agreed, his voice barely above a whisper. "Let's play."

Hilary's smile widened, and she took his hand, leading him towards the bedroom. As they entered, she closed the door, sealing them in a private world of their own creation. Brandon's heart pounded as he watched her move across the room, her hips swaying seductively. She turned, her eyes sparkling with mischief.

"Welcome home, honey," she said, her voice low and sultry. "I've been waiting for you."

Brandon felt his throat constrict as he tried to play along. "I'm home, my love. I missed you so much."

Hilary giggled, a playful sound that sent shivers down his spine. "Oh, really? Then come and show me how much you've missed me."

She moved closer, her fingers trailing along his chest, and Brandon's breath caught as she undid the buttons of his jacket, one by one, exposing his muscular torso. Her touch was like fire on his skin, and he couldn't resist the urge to pull her close, crushing her soft body against his.

"You're so strong," she murmured, her lips brushing against his neck. "I love how you make me feel safe, even in this crazy world."

Brandon's hands slid down her back, cupping her curves through the fabric of her dress. "You're incredible, Hilary. I never imagined I'd find someone like you."

She pressed her body against his, her breasts pushing against his chest. "And I never thought I'd be so turned on by a nerdy accountant," she teased, her breath hot on his skin. "But you're so much more than that, Brandon."

He chuckled, his hands moving to the zipper at the back of her dress. "Oh yeah? And what am I, then?"

"You're my hero," she whispered, her voice thick with desire. "My protector, my lover. And tonight, you're my husband."

With a swift motion, Brandon unzipped her dress, letting it fall to the floor, revealing her body in all its glory. Hilary stood before him in a lacy black bra and matching panties, her curves accentuated by the lingerie. Brandon's eyes feasted on her, his desire burning hotter with each passing moment.

"You're beautiful," he breathed, his hands moving to cup her breasts, his thumbs brushing over her erect nipples.

Hilary arched into his touch, her head falling back as a soft moan escaped her lips. "I'm yours, Brandon. Take me."

He lowered her onto the bed, his body covering hers, and they kissed passionately, their tongues dancing in a sensual rhythm. Brandon's hands explored her body, caressing her soft skin, his touch both tender and demanding. He unhooked her bra, freeing her breasts, and lowered his head to suckle her nipples, eliciting a chorus of moans from Hilary.

"Brandon, please," she pleaded, her hands gripping his shoulders. "I need you inside me."

He obliged, sliding his hands beneath her panties, feeling the heat and wetness between her thighs. With one swift motion, he tore away the flimsy fabric, baring her completely to his gaze. Hilary's pussy glistened with desire, her lips parted in invitation.

Brandon positioned himself between her legs, his dick throbbing with anticipation. He entered her slowly, savoring the sensation of her tight walls enveloping him. Hilary gasped, her nails digging into his back as he filled her completely.

"Oh God, yes," she cried out, her hips rising to meet his thrusts. "Fuck me, Brandon. Make me forget everything but you."

He obliged, his hips moving in a steady rhythm, each stroke driving deeper, harder. Hilary's cries filled the room, a symphony of pleasure and need. Brandon's own desire threatened to overwhelm him, but he held on, determined to give her the ultimate pleasure.

"Ride me, baby," he grunted, flipping them over so that Hilary was on top. "Show me how much you want it."

Hilary straddled his waist, her hands gripping his shoulders for balance. She rose and fell, impaling herself on his shaft, her breasts bouncing with each movement. Brandon's hands grasped her hips, guiding her as she rode him with abandon, her eyes closed in ecstasy.

"That's it, baby," he growled, his voice thick with desire. "You're so fucking hot. Take what you need."

Hilary's moans filled the room as she found her release, her pussy clenching around his shaft. Brandon's own orgasm was close, his balls tightening with each thrust. He wanted to prolong this moment, but his body had other ideas.

"I'm gonna cum, Hilary," he warned, his breath coming in short gasps.

"Yes, Brandon," she cried, her nails digging into his chest. "Cum for me, inside me. Fill me with your love."

Her words were like a trigger, and Brandon's release surged through him, his dick throbbing as he emptied himself deep within her. Hilary's body trembled as she climaxed again, her pussy milking his spent cock. They collapsed in a tangle of limbs, their hearts pounding in unison.

In the aftermath of their passionate encounter, they lay entwined, their bodies still glowing with satisfaction. Brandon's hands stroked Hilary's hair, his eyes filled with love and admiration.

"That was incredible," he whispered, his voice hoarse with emotion. "I never knew sex could be like this."

Hilary smiled, her fingers tracing patterns on his chest. "Me neither. It's like we're meant to be together, Brandon. Like we complete each other."

He nodded, his heart swelling with love. "I've been thinking about our future, about what comes after the war. I want to build a life with you, Hilary. I want us to have a family."

Her eyes widened, a mixture of surprise and joy. "Really? Brandon, I... I want that too. I can't imagine my life without you in it."

Brandon took a deep breath, gathering his courage. "Then marry me, Hilary. Let's make a life together, no matter what the future holds."

Hilary's eyes glistened with tears as she threw her arms around him, her kiss sealing their unspoken promise. "Yes, Brandon. Yes, I will."

In that moment, as they held each other in the quiet house, they knew their love would sustain them through the darkest of times. The war raged on outside, but within the walls of that abandoned home, Brandon and Hilary had found a sanctuary, a place where their love could grow and flourish, even in the face of adversity.

As they prepared to leave, their mission forgotten for a while, they knew their bond had been strengthened by their shared passion. The war had brought them together, but it was their love that would carry them through, giving them the strength to fight for a brighter future—a future where they could build a life, a family, and a home, free from the shadows of war.

Virginia Beach awaited its liberation, and Brandon and Hilary, now engaged, were ready to face the challenges ahead, their love a beacon of hope in the darkness.

Chapter 12

The sun was setting over Virginia Beach, casting an orange hue across the camp as Brandon and Hilary made their way back from their scouting mission. The day had been intense, filled with stealthy maneuvers and careful observations of the Russian base. They had gathered crucial information, and now it was time to debrief their CO and prepare for the impending assault.

Entering the command tent, Brandon and Hilary found Sergeant Johnson deep in thought, studying a map of the city. The CO looked up, his eyes narrowing in concentration. "Report," he demanded, his voice sharp and focused. Brandon, always the composed one, stepped forward, his tall, muscular frame filling the space.

"Sir, the Russian base is heavily fortified. They've set up multiple layers of defense, including barbed wire and sniper nests. We believe they have a significant number of troops stationed there, sir." Brandon's intelligence shone through as he provided a detailed account of their findings.

Hilary, standing by his side, added, "We managed to identify a weak spot in their perimeter, sir. A blind spot in their patrol route. We think if we hit them there, we might be able to breach their defenses." Sergeant Johnson nodded, his eyes fixed on the map.

"Good work, soldiers. Your insights are invaluable. We'll launch the assault at dawn. Get some rest; it's going to be a long night and an even longer day tomorrow." The CO's tone was grave, knowing the risks they were about to undertake.

Brandon and Hilary exchanged a glance, a silent communication filled with unspoken words. They knew the dangers ahead, but their bond had grown stronger with each challenge they faced. As they left the tent, the weight of their mission settled upon them.

Back at their squad's tent, the weary soldiers were preparing for the night. Brandon and Hilary shared a cot, their private space within the bustling camp. As they lay down, the events of the day began to catch up with them. Brandon, his brown eyes filled with determination, turned to Hilary.

"We're really doing this, Hil. Taking on the Russians head-first. It's crazy, but I believe we can make a difference." Hilary, her brown hair framing her beautiful face, smiled at him.

"We've made it this far, Bran. Together. We're a team, and we'll fight side by side. I trust you, and I know we can do this." Her words were like a balm to his soul, easing the tension in his body.

Brandon's eyes softened as he reached out to caress her cheek. "I love you, Hilary. I'm so glad I found you in this mess. You're my rock, my light in the darkness." Hilary's heart swelled with emotion, and she leaned in, capturing his lips in a tender kiss. Their love, a beacon in the midst of war, was a force that kept them going.

"I love you too, Brandon. And I want to be with you, no matter what happens tomorrow," she whispered against his lips. Brandon's heart raced, and he pulled her close, their bodies intertwining.

"We should get some rest, but I can't help but want to feel you, one last time before we face the Russians," Hilary said, her voice laced with desire. Brandon hesitated, glancing around the tent.

"But Hil, we're sharing this space with the others. We can't..." He trailed off, not wanting to deny her, yet mindful of their surroundings.

Hilary's playful side emerged, her eyes sparkling with mischief. "Who says we need to make noise? I want to feel you inside me, Brandon, but I don't want to wait until tomorrow. We might not get another chance." She reached for his hand, placing it on her thigh. Brandon's breath quickened as he felt her warmth through the thin fabric of her pants.

"Okay, but we have to be quiet. Our squad mates are right here," he whispered, his voice hoarse with desire. Hilary nodded, her fingers working quickly to unbuckle his belt. She pulled down his pants, her eyes fixed on his growing erection. With a soft groan, Brandon leaned back, allowing her to take control.

Hilary stroked his length, her touch firm and confident. She knew how to pleasure him, and soon, Brandon's breath became shallow, his body tensing with arousal. As she jerked him off, her other hand slipped under her tank top, teasing her own nipples. Brandon's eyes locked onto her, his desire for her evident.

"I want you, Hil. Now," he growled, his voice husky. Hilary positioned herself on her side, facing away from him. She reached behind, guiding his throbbing cock to her wet entrance. With a gentle push, Brandon slid into her, filling her from behind.

They both bit their lips to stifle their moans as Brandon began to thrust slowly, his hips moving in a steady rhythm. Hilary's hands clutched the blanket beneath her, her knuckles turning white as she tried to muffle her pleasure. The sensation of being filled by Brandon was exquisite, and she couldn't help but move against him, meeting his thrusts.

Brandon's hands grasped her hips, guiding her movements, ensuring their rhythm remained quiet yet intense. He leaned forward, his lips brushing her neck, sending shivers down her spine. "You feel so good, baby," he whispered, his breath hot against her skin.

Hilary's body was on fire, her senses heightened by the clandestine nature of their lovemaking. She could feel her orgasm building, her core tightening around Brandon's shaft. "Brandon, I'm close," she whispered, her voice shaking.

He understood her need, and with a few precise, deep thrusts, he sent her over the edge. Hilary's body trembled as waves of pleasure washed over her. She bit down on the blanket, her muffled cry a testament to the intensity of her release. Brandon continued to move within her, his own desire building to a fever pitch.

As Hilary's orgasm subsided, Brandon's pace quickened, his control slipping. He pulled out, his cock glistening with their combined juices, and positioned himself at her entrance once more. This time, he thrust into her with urgency, his need for release overwhelming. Hilary cried out softly, her body welcoming him, matching his passion.

The sound of their flesh slapping together filled the tent, but their squad mates, exhausted from the day's activities, remained oblivious. Brandon's hands gripped Hilary's hips tightly, his fingers digging into her soft flesh as he pounded into her.

"I'm gonna cum, Hil," he whispered hoarsely, his breath hot against her ear. Hilary reached between her legs, finding her clit, and began to rub in time with his thrusts.

"Yes, Brandon, cum for me," she urged, her own desire rising again. Brandon's body tensed, and with a guttural groan, he spilled his seed deep inside her, his release intense and satisfying. Hilary's fingers quickened on her clit, and she followed him over the edge, her orgasm rippling through her body.

They lay entwined, their hearts racing, as they caught their breath. Brandon gently withdrew from her, and they quickly redressed, straightening their clothes and composure. The tent was quiet once more, as if their passionate encounter had never happened.

Brandon pulled Hilary close, his strong arms wrapping around her. "I love you, Hilary Tork. No matter what happens tomorrow, remember that," he whispered, his lips brushing her forehead.

Hilary smiled, her eyes glistening with unshed tears. "I love you too, Brandon Hill. And I'll be by your side, always." They held each other tightly, their love a shield against the uncertainties of war. As they drifted off to sleep, their minds were filled with thoughts of each other, their bond unbreakable.

The night passed, and the faint light of dawn crept into the tent. Brandon and Hilary, now rested and refreshed, prepared for the battle ahead. They knew the risks, but their love had given them the strength to face whatever awaited them. As they joined their squad, ready to launch the assault, their hearts were filled with determination and a love that would carry them through the firefight to come.

The future of Virginia Beach hung in the balance, and Brandon and Hilary, united in love and purpose, were ready to fight for their city and for each other.

Chapter 13

As the sun began to set over Virginia Beach, Brandon and Hilary prepared for the most crucial battle of their lives. The city, once a vibrant tourist destination, now lay in ruins, a testament to the devastation of war. The Russian forces had occupied the eastern district, turning it into a fortified base, and it was time to take it back. The couple's love had blossomed amidst the chaos, providing them with the strength and courage to face the challenges ahead.

Brandon, with his strategic mind and leadership skills, had earned the respect of his fellow soldiers. He gathered his squad, a group of brave men and women who shared his determination, and outlined the plan. "We'll launch a surprise attack at midnight," he explained, his voice steady and confident. "The element of surprise will be our greatest weapon. We hit them hard, and we hit them fast. Our goal is to capture the main command post and cripple their defenses."

Hilary, her eyes sparkling with determination, stood by Brandon's side. She had proven herself time and again as a skilled nurse and a formidable fighter. Her expertise in medicine had saved countless lives, and her ability to stay calm under pressure made her an invaluable asset. "We'll need to be swift and precise," she added, her voice carrying a hint of her southern accent. "The Russians won't expect us, but they won't go down without a fight. We must be ready for anything."

The squad nodded in agreement, their faces a mix of excitement and apprehension. They knew the risks, but the chance to liberate their city was worth every danger. As the group prepared their gear, loading magazines and checking their weapons, Brandon pulled Hilary aside, taking a moment to appreciate the woman he loved.

"Are you ready for this?" he asked, his dark eyes searching hers.

Hilary smiled, her freckles standing out against her pale skin. "I'm always ready when I'm with you," she replied, her voice soft and sincere. "We've been through so much together, and our love has only grown stronger. We'll face this battle like we've faced everything else—together."

Brandon leaned in and kissed her gently, their lips meeting in a moment of tender passion. "You're my strength, Hilary. I wouldn't want to do this with anyone else. Just promise me you'll stay safe."

"I promise," she whispered, her hands resting on his broad shoulders. "But you be careful too, Brandon. We have a future to build together."

The couple shared a private moment, their love a beacon of light in the darkness of war. They had found solace in each other, and their bond was unbreakable. As they prepared to embark on the dangerous mission, they knew that their love would be their greatest weapon.

Midnight approached, and the squad moved into position under the cover of darkness. The Russian base loomed ahead, its walls illuminated by floodlights, casting eerie shadows across the deserted streets. Brandon, leading the charge, signaled for the attack to begin.

The squad stormed the base, their weapons blazing. Flash bangs exploded, disorienting the enemy, and the sound of gunfire echoed through the night. Hilary, her rifle at the ready, moved with precision, taking cover behind a crumbling wall. She fired at the Russians, her aim true, as she defended her position.

Brandon, his muscular frame moving with agility, darted from one cover to another, eliminating targets with calculated shots. The battle raged on, and the Russians, caught off guard, scrambled to respond. Hilary heard a shout and turned to see Brandon engaging a group of enemy soldiers. She fired in support, taking down two Russians who were about to flank him.

"Thanks, Hil!" Brandon shouted, his eyes scanning the battlefield. "Keep an eye on that sniper nest. We need to take them out!"

Hilary nodded, her heart pounding as she spotted the glint of a sniper scope. She fired a quick burst, forcing the sniper to retreat. The fighting intensified, and the squad pushed forward, capturing key positions. But the Russians were not going down without a fight.

As Hilary reloaded her rifle, a burst of gunfire caught her off guard. She felt a searing pain in her shoulder, and her body slumped against the wall. "Hilary!" Brandon cried out, his voice filled with panic. He rushed to her side, his heart pounding as he saw the blood staining her shirt.

"I'm okay," she managed to say, her voice weak. "Just a scratch. Keep fighting, Brandon. We're almost there."

Brandon's eyes blazed with determination. "No, we're getting you out of here. We'll fall back and regroup."

"No, we can't!" Hilary insisted, her voice rising. "We're so close. I can hold them off. You go, take the command post. I'll cover you."

Brandon's face contorted with emotion. He knew Hilary was hurt, and the thought of leaving her was unbearable. But he also understood the importance of their mission. "I can't leave you, Hil. We're in this together."

"I'm not going anywhere," she said firmly, her eyes locking with his. "I'm your wife, remember? I'll defend this position until you come back for me."

Brandon's heart ached as he realized the depth of Hilary's commitment. He knew she was right; they had to keep fighting. "Alright, we'll do this together," he said, his voice hoarse with emotion. "But we need to move. We're sitting ducks here."

Hilary nodded, gritting her teeth against the pain. Brandon helped her to her feet, and they advanced, taking cover behind a pile of rubble. The Russians were pushing back, their numbers overwhelming. Brandon fired his rifle, his shots finding their targets, but the enemy kept coming.

Suddenly, a hail of bullets rained down on their position. Hilary's breath caught in her throat as she saw Brandon's body jerk with each impact. He slumped to the ground, his eyes wide with shock. "Brandon!" she screamed, her voice filled with anguish.

"I'm hit," he gasped, his hand reaching for her. "But I'm not going anywhere. We'll hold them off."

Hilary's heart raced as she realized they were both injured and surrounded. The Russians were closing in, their victory seemingly assured. "We can't let them win," she said, her voice fierce. "We fought too hard for this city."

Brandon managed a weak smile. "Then we fight till the end. Together."

As if in response to their determination, the sound of rotor blades cut through the night sky. Hilary and Brandon looked up, their eyes widening in surprise. American attack helicopters appeared, their guns blazing, providing much-needed air support. The Russians, caught in the crossfire, scattered, their resistance crumbling.

Hilary and Brandon, despite their injuries, continued to fight, their spirits lifted by the arrival of reinforcements. The squad rallied, pushing forward with renewed vigor. Hilary, her rifle steady, took down enemy soldiers, her aim fueled by adrenaline and love. Brandon, summoning his last reserves of strength, rose to his feet and fired a rocket-propelled grenade, destroying a Russian armored vehicle.

The battle raged on, but the tide had turned. The American forces, with the element of surprise and the support of the helicopters, overwhelmed the Russians. The enemy began to retreat, their once-stronghold falling to the determined squad.

Hilary, her body trembling with exhaustion and pain, made her way to Brandon's side. He lay on the ground, his breathing labored, but his eyes sparkled with determination. "We did it," he whispered, his hand reaching for hers.

"We did," she agreed, her voice choked with emotion. "We won, Brandon. We took back our city."

Brandon smiled, his eyes filled with love and pride. "We did it together, Hil. Just like we always do."

The couple shared a moment of triumph and relief, their love a shining beacon in the aftermath of battle. The helicopters landed, and medical teams rushed to their aid. Hilary refused to leave Brandon's side, insisting they be treated together.

As the sun rose over the liberated city, the squad gathered, their faces weary but triumphant. Virginia Beach had been reclaimed, and the Russians had been pushed back. Brandon and Hilary, their love a symbol of hope and resilience, had played a pivotal role in the victory.

Chapter 14

As the sun cast its warm rays over the now peaceful city of Virginia Beach, Brandon Hill and Hilary Tork found themselves in a hospital room, their bodies bruised and battered from the intense battle they had just fought. The city had finally been liberated, and the sounds of celebration and relief echoed through the streets. Brandon, his muscular frame now adorned with bandages, lay in his bed, his dark eyes gleaming with satisfaction. He had led his squad with unwavering determination, and their efforts had paid off. Hilary, her curvy figure wrapped in a hospital gown, sat by his side, her hand intertwined with his. She had been his rock throughout the mission, her nursing skills proving invaluable on the battlefield. Their love, forged in the crucible of war, had become an unbreakable bond.

The hospital room was filled with the aroma of fresh flowers, sent by grateful citizens who had heard tales of the heroic couple's exploits. Brandon and Hilary had become local legends, their story spreading like wildfire across the city. They had not only fought for Virginia Beach but had also embodied the spirit of resilience and love in the face of adversity. As they rested, their wounds slowly healing, they couldn't help but reflect on the extraordinary journey that had brought them to this moment.

A gentle knock on the door interrupted their quiet contemplation. Sergeant Johnson, their commanding officer, entered the room, his weathered face creased with a mixture of concern and admiration. "How are my two heroes doing today?" he asked, his voice filled with warmth. Brandon and Hilary exchanged glances, their eyes sparkling with mischief.

"We're doing well, Sergeant," Brandon replied, his deep voice soft but confident. "The doctors say we'll be up and about in no time. We just need a little rest after all the excitement."

Hilary, ever the life of the party, added, "And we've got plenty to celebrate, haven't we, Brandon? Virginia Beach is free, and we played our part in making it happen." Her brown eyes shone with pride, and her playful smile lit up the room.

Sergeant Johnson chuckled, his stern demeanor softening. "You two certainly did. Your bravery and skills on the battlefield have not gone unnoticed. The city owes you a great debt of gratitude." He paused, his eyes growing serious. "In fact, I've been authorized to offer you both a unique opportunity. With the Russians retreating and the city secure, the US Army is looking to expand its ranks. I've been asked to recruit exceptional individuals like yourselves."

Brandon and Hilary exchanged a look of surprise. Joining the US Army was an opportunity many soldiers dreamed of, a chance to serve their country on a larger scale. However, their hearts were deeply rooted in Virginia Beach, the place they had fought so hard to protect.

"Sergeant, we're honored by the offer," Brandon began, his voice sincere. "But Virginia Beach is our home. We've built something special here, and we want to stay and help rebuild. The militia has become our family, and we believe we can make a difference right here."

Hilary nodded in agreement, her expression resolute. "We've seen the worst of war, and now we want to be a part of the healing process. The people of this city have shown us so much love and support. We'd like to give back and ensure Virginia Beach rises stronger than ever."

Sergeant Johnson understood their decision, his respect for them growing even more. "I respect your choice, and I know the city will benefit greatly from your dedication. The militia will be lucky to have you both. You've proven your worth as soldiers and as leaders."

He turned to leave, but before he reached the door, Brandon's voice stopped him. "Sergeant, there's something else we wanted to tell you. Something that makes our decision even more certain."

Intrigued, Sergeant Johnson turned back, his eyes curious. "What is it, son?"

Brandon's voice was filled with emotion as he looked at Hilary, his love for her evident in his gaze. "We're getting married, Sergeant. Hilary and I want to build a life together here in Virginia Beach. This city has become our home, and we want to be a part of its future."

The room fell silent for a moment, as if the weight of their decision hung in the air. Then, Sergeant Johnson smiled, a wide grin spreading across his face. "Well, I'll be darned! Congratulations, you two! That's wonderful news. I can't think of a better way to start a new chapter in this city's history."

He extended his hand, and Brandon and Hilary shook it firmly. "The US Army's loss is Virginia Beach's gain. I wish you both all the happiness in the world. And remember, if you ever need anything, the Army will always be there for you."

With a final salute, Sergeant Johnson left the room, leaving Brandon and Hilary alone, their hearts filled with joy and anticipation. They had faced the horrors of war, fought side by side, and now they had a future to look forward to—a future together.

As the afternoon sun bathed their room in a golden glow, Brandon leaned over and gently kissed Hilary's hand. "I love you, Hilary. I can't wait to spend the rest of my life with you, building a home here in Virginia Beach."

Hilary's eyes glistened with tears of happiness. "I love you too, Brandon. This city has become our sanctuary, and together, we'll make it even more beautiful. We'll start a family, raise our kids here, and show them the power of love and resilience."

Their love story, born in the shadows of war, had blossomed into a beacon of hope and determination. Virginia Beach, once a battleground, would now witness the growth of their love, a love that had survived the darkest of times.

The days that followed were filled with happiness and excitement. Brandon and Hilary's engagement became public knowledge, and the city rejoiced in their newfound peace and the prospect of a joyous wedding. The militia, now a well-oiled machine, continued to maintain order and assist in the city's reconstruction.

Brandon and Hilary threw themselves into the rebuilding efforts, organizing community events and fundraisers to support those who had lost their homes and loved ones. They became symbols of unity and strength, their presence bringing comfort and hope to the citizens.

As the weeks turned into months, Virginia Beach underwent a remarkable transformation. The scars of war began to fade, replaced by new buildings, thriving businesses, and a sense of community. Brandon and Hilary's wedding day arrived, and the city came together to celebrate their love.

The ceremony was held on the beach, the setting sun painting the sky with vibrant hues. Friends, family, and fellow militia members gathered, their joy palpable. Brandon and Hilary exchanged vows, promising to love and support each other through the good times and the bad.

As they kissed beneath the setting sun, the city erupted in cheers, fireworks lighting up the night sky. Virginia Beach had not only survived the war but had also emerged stronger, united by the love and courage of its people.

Brandon and Hilary's story became a legend, inspiring generations to come. Their love, a beacon in the darkness, proved that even in the midst of war, beauty and hope could prevail. As they built their lives together, the city flourished, a testament to the power of love and the resilience of the human spirit.

And so, their journey continued, not just as soldiers but as a couple deeply in love, ready to face the challenges of life, knowing that their bond would carry them through. Virginia Beach, the city they had fought for, would forever be their home, a place where their love story began and where their future awaited.

Don't miss out!

Visit the website below and you can sign up to receive emails whenever Michael Gordon publishes a new book. There's no charge and no obligation.

https://books2read.com/r/B-A-KEXRC-VYZHF

Did you love *Love & War: The Battle of Virginia Beach*? Then you should read *Will You Marry Me?*[1] by Michael Gordon!

[2]

The sun-kissed shores of Virginia Beach played host to a unique social experiment, a reality TV show that aimed to bring two strangers together in the hope of finding love. Among the eager participants were Zayden Moss, a charismatic former athlete, and Sabrina Chun, a reserved nurse with a rebellious streak. Their paths were about to collide in the most unexpected way, and the cameras were there to capture every moment. In the end of the experiment, will they stay married or be divorced? Find out in this season of Will you Marry Me?

---

1. https://books2read.com/u/4AlJdk

2. https://books2read.com/u/4AlJdk

Also by Michael Gordon

Will You Marry Me?
Love & War: The Battle of Virginia Beach

About the Author

Michael Gordon is a modern romance author who enjoys writing steamy, heart racing, interracial romances. When he's not writing, he's reading other swoon worthy interracial romance stories, traveling with his wife & kids, or watching sports.

www.ingramcontent.com/pod-product-compliance
Lightning Source LLC
LaVergne TN
LVHW091123150826
845673LV00002B/957

* 9 7 9 8 2 2 7 4 9 6 8 8 1 *